# GEEK
# GUARDIANS

# GEEK
# GUARDIANS
## RECESS REVOLUTION

Michael Fry

Silver Dolphin

**Silver Dolphin Books**
An imprint of Printers Row Publishing Group
A division of Readerlink Distribution Services, LLC
9717 Pacific Heights Blvd, San Diego, CA 92121
www.silverdolphinbooks.com

Printers Row Publishing Group is a division of
Readerlink Distribution Services, LLC.
Silver Dolphin Books is a registered trademark of
Readerlink Distribution Services, LLC.

All notations of errors or omissions should be addressed to
Silver Dolphin Books, Editorial Department, at the above
address.

Originally published as *Odd Squad: Bully Bait*.

ISBN: 978-1-6672-0028-6
Manufactured, printed, and assembled in Guangzhou, China.
First printing, January 2022. GD/01/22
26 25 24 23 22  1 2 3 4 5

# FOR KIM
It had to be you

# CHAPTER 1

I was stuffed in my locker.

Again.

It wasn't so bad. Lockers are a lot roomier than you'd think.

Especially when you're as short as I am. I might be the shortest twelve-year-old on the planet. Which would be cool if they kept world records for that sort of thing. But they don't. I checked.

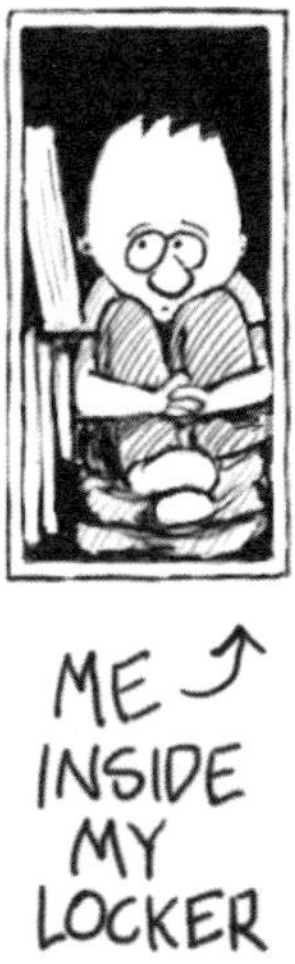


Mom says to me all the time, "Nicholas, you'll grow eventually."

*Eventually* is a Mom word that means between now and never.

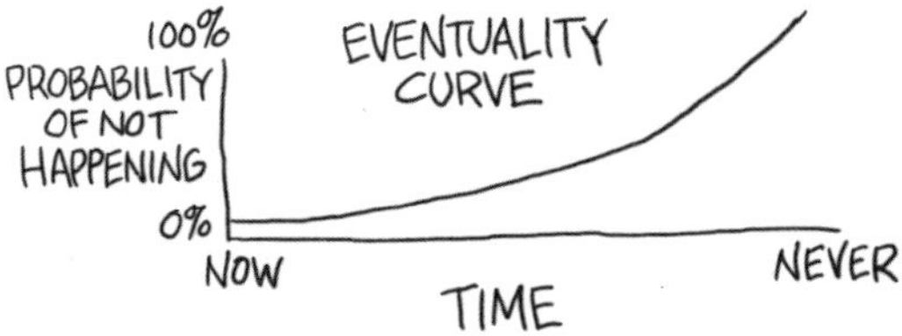

Mom's just trying to cheer me up. Which is fine. What's not fine is when she calls m Nicholas. My name is Nick. *Nicholas* sounds like some kid with head lice on Memaw's favorite show, *Dr. Holmes.*

Memaw doesn't think I'm short. She says, "You're just stuck that way 'cause when you were four you were so cute we stacked bricks on your head so you'd never grow up. You'll get unstuck. Eventually."

Memaw makes up a lot of stuff that almost makes sense but not quite.

The fact is, I'm short. Which is exactly why Roy stuffed me in my locker in the first place.

I fit.

Roy has issues. At least that's what Dr. Daniels, the school counselor, says. The only issue I see is: Roy is a mutant troll.

Unlike me, Dr. Daniels doesn't have troll-vision. She says Roy is just a regular kid who feels powerless and gets control by controlling me. She's full of beans. Roy is just mean. Some kids are, you know.

Even though I felt safe in my locker, it wasn't exactly comfortable. My butt had fallen asleep. Living-dead asleep. It's called zombie butt. And as everyone knows, zombie butt leads to log legs. You can sort of move with log legs.

But not really.

I knew if I didn't get out of that locker soon, I wasn't getting out at all. And I really didn't want to have to wait for a certain *someone* to come along to help me out.

# CHAPTER 2

It was the janitor, Mr. Dupree, staring into my locker. He was the someone I didn't want to find me. Mostly because he's weird, but also because he would make me go see Dr. Daniels in the office.

Mr. Dupree isn't weird like all grown-ups are weird. He's way weirder. I think he's a hippie. Like Memaw when she was young. Hippies are dinosaur versions of skaters.

50 MILLION YEARS AGO

TODAY

After he opened the locker, Mr. Dupree stood there for a few seconds. Then he said, "You seem to like it in there."

I shrugged. The shrug is my go-to move when anything I say may be used against me later.

"Because I find you in there a lot," he said

I shrugged again.

HOW TO SHRUG

"You want to tell me how you got in there?"

I shrugged a third time.

"Shrug, you're not going to tell me? Or shrug, you don't know how you got in there?"

I shrugged a fourth time. A new world record! Woo-hoo!

Mr. Dupree wasn't impressed. "Then I guess it must have been Emily."

I guess I must have looked surprised because he added, "Nick, I've been at Emily Dickinson Middle School a long time."

Emily isn't real. At least, I don't *think* she's real. And she's definitely not the ghost of Emily Dickinson, the poet. Kids invented her years ago to explain all the weird stuff that happens at school.

Like, why do the last five minutes of class always seem to take forever? It's Emily (she holds back the minute hand). Why does the cafeteria serve beets (which no kid has ever eaten in the history of the universe)? Emily again (she's a beet freak). Who sets up the toilet paper dispensers so that only one teeny-tiny sheet comes out at a time? That's right—Emily (sometimes she's just mean).

Emily gets around. But she didn't shove me into my locker. And I was not about to tell anyone who did.

Mr. Dupree shook his head, then reached in and pulled me out of the locker. That's when we both noticed the huge rip down the side of my shirt.

"Emily again?" Mr. Dupree asked.

No shrug this time. You can't do five shrugs.

Five shrugs, and adults go from *thinking* you're messing with them to *knowing* you're messing with them.

I shook my head no.

The shirt must have ripped when Roy stuffed me into the locker. Mom's going to notice. Shrugs and head-shakes don't work on Mom. I'll have to come up with some excuse. It can't be something lame like the dog did it or shirt-ripping aliens tried to abduct me at recess. And I can't blame it on Emily. It's not her style.

I tucked in my shirt to hide the rip as we started toward the office. Luckily, homeroom had already started, so the halls were empty. You never want to do the Wimp Walk to the office in front of an audience.

14

I like to keep my mouth shut during these walks. Anything I say is always used against me.

Unfortunately, that day Mr. Dupree wanted to chat. Out of the blue, he asked me if I'd ever been to Borneo.

I shook my head no.

Mr. Dupree told me Borneo is an island in the Pacific Ocean. It's mostly rain forests and snakes. Big snakes. Thirty-foot-long snakes. Lots of big, thirty-foot-long, kid-eating snakes.

Mr. Dupree said he was once in Borneo under deep cover—like he was some sort of spy or something. Mr. Dupree doesn't look like any spy I've ever seen. Spies are cool. Mr. Dupree is not cool.

Mr. Dupree was helping stop some tribe from being bullied by another tribe that was stealing their pigs. He said the other tribe wanted the pigs to feed to the snakes so the snakes wouldn't eat them, because . . .

. . . they were tiny little hobbit people.

SNAKE

TINY LITTLE HOBBIT PERSON

Mr. Dupree said the hobbit people were fierce warriors. They hunted in packs and took down elephants.

To feed to the snakes.

I did a report on elephants once. They only live in Africa and India. I turned to Mr. Dupree and said, "There aren't any elephants in Borneo."

"There aren't." He smiled. "Anymore."

He continued with his story. He explained that every day, a couple of hobbit people would come to steal the pigs, and he would beat them back. But one night *all* the hobbit people came.

"I could ninja maybe three or four of them, but after that it was gonna be Dupree-on-a-Stick," he said.

Even though I didn't believe a word he was saying, I had to give Mr. Dupree props for telling a good story.

"What happened next?" I asked.

"What does every bully fear?"

"I dunno," I said.

"They fear losing control."

I was confused.

Mr. Dupree said, "If they lose control, they get afraid. If they get afraid, they run away."

"How do you make them lose control?" I asked.

"You take it from them."

"How?"

Mr. Dupree smiled as he leaned down and got right in my face. He said, "You bring the crazy."

And then—right there in the middle of the hallway—Mr. Dupree brought the crazy.

HAND SMACKED

MADE MOOSE CALLS

YELLED AT MOLE PEOPLE AT CENTER OF THE EARTH

COME INTO THE LIGHT!

ARM FARTED "GREENSLEEVES"

PERFORMED SOCK PUPPET SHAKESPEARE

HARK! SHE SPEAKS!

OUT! DAMN'D SPOT!

I'd never seen a grown-up freak out like that. You'd think I would be scared, but it was really sort of awesome.

And it did the trick. "Bringing the crazy scared the hobbit people away. The tribe kept their pigs," explained Mr. Dupree.

I guess the hobbit people kept getting eaten by snakes. Mr. Dupree didn't say.

"Wait," I said. "Acting like an insane person will somehow keep me from getting stuffed in my locker?"

Mr. Dupree said, "If you scare yourself, you'll probably scare them. You can do anything crazy or scary. The scarier the better. But never pee your pants. That's just gross."

I nodded, even though I didn't believe "bringing the crazy" would work on a bully. An arm fart concert wouldn't stop Roy.

I said, "None of that stuff really happened, did it?"

"You don't believe me?"

"You're a janitor, not a spy."

"'There are more things in heaven and earth, Horatio, than are dreamt of in your philosophy.'"

"Um . . . my name is Nick."

"Nick, maybe it's true and maybe it isn't. But just because I might be lying, doesn't mean I'm not telling the truth."

Huh? How can a lie be the truth?

We arrived at the office. Dr. Daniels wasn't there. Mr. Dupree told me to sit and wait. He started to leave, then stopped and pulled a sock out of his pocket and put it on his hand.

THOUGH THIS BE MADNESS, YET THERE IS METHOD IN IT.

I told you he was weird.

# CHAPTER 3

After Mr. Dupree left, I looked around and realized I was alone. Mrs. Korn, the office secretary who everyone says is an alien, must have been on her break.

Which meant I was unsupervised. I had the whole office to myself, including the PA system.

Just as I was about to get into even more trouble, *she* showed up. *She* is Becky Harrison, the prettiest girl in school. And my girlfriend.

Sort of.

A while back, Memaw and I watched this Science Channel thing about how there might be lots and lots of universes with lots and lots of versions of everyone walking around, so that across all the universes every possible thing happens at every possible moment.

I figure in at least one of those multiple universes Becky Harrison is my girlfriend.

ONE GIGAZILLIONTH OF ALL POSSIBLE UNIVERSES

UNIVERSE WHERE BECKY IS MY GIRLFRIEND

I love science.

Becky was delivering attendance sheets. She didn't see me at first. Which was good. It gave me time to activate my cloaking device.

When I decloaked, Becky was gone. Which was a relief. I'm pretty sure if the Becky in this universe knew I existed, the Becky in the alternate universe would stop being my girlfriend.

Finally, Dr. Daniels showed up. She wasn't alone. She had a freakishly tall girl, and a husky kid (that's Memaw's word for fat) dressed up like a pretend police boy.

Before I could ask the husky kid if he got the belt and badge out of a cereal box, Dr. Daniels marched us all into her office.

Dr. Daniels and I go way back. She used to be my counselor at Buzz Aldrin Elementary School. She moved up to Emily Dickinson the same year I did.

I'm pretty sure she's stalking me.

Her office looks the same as the one back in grade school. Both of them were decorated by unicorns. It's all bright and shiny and filled with role-play puppets and not-so-helpful brochures.

ROLE-PLAY PUPPET
MR. GRUMPY PANTS

BROCHURES
YOUR FACE WON'T ALWAYS LOOK LIKE THIS.
EVERYBODY STINKS

After I was done throwing up a little in my mouth, Dr. Daniels walked in with our files. She dropped each one on her desk as she said our names. "Nick Ramsey."  *THUNK!* "Molly Wibble." *THUNK!* "Karl Mooney." *TH-THUNK!* Then she looked at us in turn and said, "I presume you know each other."

I'd seen Molly before. She's kinda hard to miss.

Whenever kids call her stuff like "The Molly Green Giant," she unleashes her withering stare of pity. It's like getting blasted with two laser beams of shame.

She's known all over school as The Stare Master.

I'd seen Karl around, too. Karl's one of those kids you avoid eye contact with because he'll think you want to be friends. Then he'll latch on to you with his superhuman loser grip.

Karl is also kind of an OFFline hacker. He likes to mess around with old electronic toys and rewire them.

Dr. Daniels sat on the edge of her desk and looked at me from the BFF Pose they taught her at counselor school. She said, "Nick, this is the eighth time this year you've been stuffed in a locker. Any idea how you got there?"

I shrugged.

She turned to Karl. "This is the ninth time you've been found hanging by your shorts from a coat hook. What happened?"

Karl shrugged.

She turned to Molly. "This is the seventh time you've been found sprawled in the hallway with your shoes tied together."

"Any clue as to who might have done it?" asked Dr. Daniels.

Molly shrugged.

Three out of three shrugs! Go, team!

Dr. Daniels shook her head and sighed. Then she said, "I know you're being bullied. I just don't know who's doing it. What I do know is that bullies go after isolated kids—kids who are not part of a group. And you three are definitely not part of any group."

She nodded. "You all suffer from *peer allergies*."

That didn't make any sense to me. I wasn't allergic to other kids. I just didn't like them very much.

TOP 5 REASONS I DON'T LIKE OTHER KIDS VERY MUCH

5. LAME
4. MEAN
3. DUMB
2. TALL
1. DID I MENTION TALL?

Karl raised his hand. "Does that mean we have to live in a bubble for the rest of our lives?"

Dr. Daniels said no. Karl looked really disappointed.

"You three need a place to *belong*," said Dr. Daniels.

Karl raised his hand again. "But I belong in Safety Patrol."

Dr. Daniels closed her eyes. "Karl, you're the *only* member of Safety Patrol."

That's when I realized where I'd seen that belt and badge before. I'd seen it on Karl during fire drills as he pointed at exits everyone could see for themselves.

Dr. Daniels continued, "Other kids find places to belong. Like sports, student government, band, or chorus. But not you guys. I don't understand. Why?"

That's easy, I thought: *BECAUSE THEY'RE ALL LAME!*

Sports? I thought about trying out for football until I realized the other players already have  something they can kick, hit, or punch.

They don't need me.

Clubs? I would have to stay after school to be in a club. Roy gets enough shots at me as it is. Besides, it's a waste of time! Especially the Peer Mediation Club. As if a bunch of bossy eighth-grade girls could keep Roy from shoving me into my locker. Please.

Student government? Really? They have about as much power over school as I have over Roy.

And band and chorus are okay for some kids, but they were where my dreams went to die.

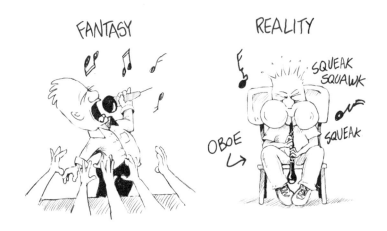

But I didn't tell Dr. Daniels any of that.

I just shrugged again while Molly looked at her shoes and Karl picked at a scab on his arm.

Dr. Daniels continued, "I'm convinced that if you three could each just find a place to belong, you wouldn't have such targets on your backs."

Hello? They weren't on our *backs*.

That's when Dr. Daniels pointed at Karl and said, "And I think I've found just such a place."

*Wait. She isn't going to say what I think she's going to say. No, please, no!* But before I could get my brain to kick my mouth into gear, Dr. Daniels announced, "Welcome to . . ."

"SAFETY PATROL?" I cried.

Dr. Daniels smiled. "Won't that be fun?"

# CHAPTER 4

I was doomed. And there was no getting out of it. When Dr. Daniels told Molly, Karl, and me to swap phone numbers so we could coordinate, we looked at her like she had two heads and one of them was on fire. That's when she told us Safety Patrol was mandatory. She was going to force us to fit in whether we liked it or not.

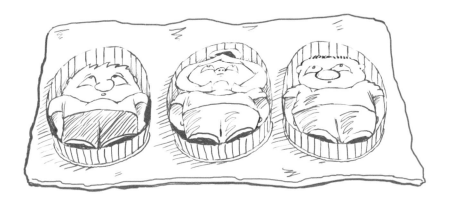

You might think things could only have gotten better, right?

Wrong.

In English class, one of the vocabulary words was *humiliated*. I didn't have any trouble using it in a sentence.

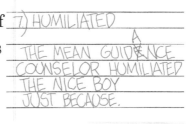
7) HUMILIATED
THE MEAN GUIDANCE COUNSELOR HUMILIATED THE NICE BOY JUST BECAUSE.

In science class, we talked about how a body in motion (like me, growing) will remain in motion unless acted upon by some other force.

In math class, we had this word problem: "If a locker is 3' x 1' x 1', how many books 3" x 12" x 8" can fit in the locker?" The answer was four—at least for any locker I'm stuffed in.

But the worst happened after school.

I was hiding behind a tree waiting for Roy to get on his bus so that I could get on *my* bus without being hassled.

I looked everywhere, but I couldn't find him. Or smell him (Roy uses a lot of body spray).

Eventually, I caught a whiff of grapefruit chocolate musk, and about minute or so later, I saw Roy.

He was walking toward his bus when he suddenly stopped . . . and officially made this THE WORST DAY OF MY LIFE!

Roy stopped to talk to BECKY! He can't do that! Didn't he know she's MY alternate universe girlfriend?

My heart sank, my shoulders sagged, and my knees gave way. I collapsed and immediately asked . . .

DID I JUST LIE DOWN IN AN ANT MOUND?

# CHAPTER 5

First, my busybody guidance counselor sentences me to a life of loserdom. Next, my sworn enemy dares to speak to my alternate universe girlfriend. Then, I get covered in ant bites. And finally, I get home from school, and Mom yells at me for leaving the milk out.

Our bull terrier knocked the carton of milk off the counter when she was counter-surfing. Janice and milk do not mix. Now she'll be farting for days.

My life stinks. And it's not just Janice.

It's been like this for the last two years—since Mom and Dad split up. One second you're a kid and you're part

TOOT!

of this family, and then everything changes and you're a part of . . . what?

BEFORE PHOTOSHOP        AFTER PHOTOSHOP

It feels weird—like you're jumping off a swing, and you look down and the ground is gone. You fall. And you keep falling until you get used to it

and forget you're falling until a day like today happens . . . and you wake up and realize . . . you're still falling.

It's not all bad. Birthdays are way better after a divorce. Everyone feels sorry for you.

Also, Memaw moving in has helped a lot. It's hard to be sad with Memaw around.

For example, when I went to look for Janice to put her outside, I found that Memaw had tied one of those deodorizer trees to her tail.

If Memaw were a superhero, her superpower would be deodorizing. She wears an air-freshener in a holster on her belt.

Before I could get out of the way, Memaw started

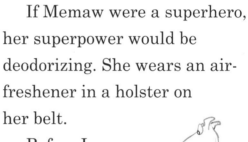

spraying at will. I fled the cloud of deodorizer fog to the dining room, where Mom was setting the table for dinner.

I was a little surprised to see Mom at home. She's a nurse, and her schedule can be sort of random. Sometimes she just sort of appears—

like a ninja—out of thin air. Keeps me on my toes. Which I'm pretty sure is why she does it.

She works in the emergency room at the hospital. This means I hear every horrible story about how some stupid kid got hurt. I'm surprised she doesn't send me to school with a Secret Service detail.

Still, Mom's pretty cool—for a mom. I can talk to her if I need to, even though I have  to be careful not to freak her out about school stuff. The last thing I need is my mom trying to protect me from Roy.

We finally sat down to eat. We were having mac and cheese with tuna. We eat a LOT of mac and cheese. We eat it with tuna, hamburger, sausage, and my favorite: baloney. We eat it because it's easy and it goes with everything, but mostly because it's the only thing Memaw will eat. It's filled with preservatives. Memaw says the preservatives are what're preserving her.

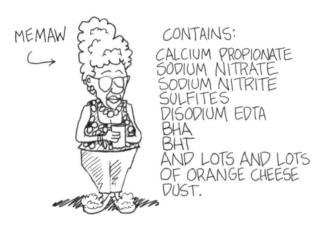

MEMAW →

CONTAINS:
CALCIUM PROPIONATE
SODIUM NITRATE
SODIUM NITRITE
SULFITES
DISODIUM EDTA
BHA
BHT
AND LOTS AND LOTS
OF ORANGE CHEESE
DUST.

About halfway through dinner, Mom asks me how my day was. Like I was really going to tell her I'm doomed and am going to have to hide in the basement for the rest of my life.

WHOMPATA! WHOMPATA!

ME IN
20
YEARS
↳

So I told her my day was "Fine."

"Fine?" she asked.

My mom has this super-annoying way of knowing when things are *not* fine. I don't know how she does it. It's some sort of psychic brain squish-squeeze thing.

My only smart response was to hit her with WTMI: Way Too Much Information. I bombarded her with lots and lots of boring WTMI about class assignments, the lunch menu, how many pencils I sharpened, how there was no toilet paper in the third stall in the first floor boys' bathroom, and the color of Dr. Daniels's shoes.

"You saw Dr. Daniels today?" she asked. "Did something happen? Why wasn't I told?"

I always forget there's such a thing as WWTMI: Way WAY Too Much Information.

I scrambled. "I saw her in the hall," I said. "Her shoes were seriously purple. Bright purple. Hurt-my-eyes purple."

Mom gave me that mom-look that says, *You can run, but you can't hide.*

"Mm-huh," she said as she spotted the rip in my shirt. "What happened there?"

I decided to play it safe and go back to basics. I shrugged.

Mom turned to Memaw and raised an eyebrow. "It's a mystery."

Memaw shook her head.  "A mystery is like a pig wearin' underwear. Don't make no sense till you see him puttin' on pants."

We all stared at one another for a second. Then Mom snorted. I giggled. And Memaw did that weird whooping thing she does. Everything was cool again . . .

. . . for about three seconds, until Memaw started choking.

Mom jumped up and slapped Memaw hard on the back. A piece of macaroni shot out of Memaw's mouth, sailed across the room, landed on the TV screen, and stuck there.

We all took a deep breath, looked at one another, and lost it. We laughed so hard, I started to think how I would miss all this if I had to hide in the basement for the rest of my life.

# CHAPTER 6

After supper I watched *Dr. Holmes* with Memaw. It was the one with the guy with the brain-eating amoebas.

I'M AFRAID WE HAVE NO CHOICE BUT TO AMPUTATE...

After Memaw fell asleep, I swiped her phone and ran to my room. I use her phone to text Roy so that I can say stuff to him I can't say as Nick Ramsey. Since Memaw's real name is Maxine, or Max for short, and shows up that way on reverse lookup, all Roy knows is that someone named Max sends him texts that really, really annoy him.

You see, I've been me my whole life. And it's okay, I guess. I mean, except for last couple years with the not-growing thing . . . and the Roy thing . . . and the Becky thing . . . and now this Safety Patrol thing.

But that's just the outside me. There's another me on the inside who's tall and strong and always smells like pie.

OUTSIDE ME          INSIDE ME

One day, I started wondering how I could get the inside me on the outside. How could I turn myself inside out?

I found the answer where all life's answers are: in my favorite comic book, *NanoNerd*.

NanoNerd was born without a spine. It wasn't until he downloaded his consciousness into the NanoBot and became the first android/nerd hybrid that he truly became himself.

Since I couldn't figure out a way to download my consciousness into a NanoBot, I figured out a simpler way to turn myself inside out.

By day, I'm Nick Ramsey: short, shy, and invisible. By night, with the help of Memaw's cell phone, I text as the tall, confident, and popular . . . Max Pounder!

Here's what I texted that night.

Nick: Hey, Roy! u r so dumb u sleep with a solar-powered night-light

Roy texted Max back:

Roy: If I ever find out who u r, I'm gonna sit on u until brains come out your nose!

As Memaw would say, it's a *hoot* to text Roy! It makes that twenty-ninth visit to Dr. Daniels's office, when I snagged her class cell phone directory, so totally worth it.

After a few more fun texts to Roy (fun for me), Max got a text from Becky. She may not know who *I* am, but she's Max's BFF.

Max and Becky have been texting for the last few weeks. She knows I go to her school because we talk about stuff that only a kid at Emily Dickinson could know, like who shot milk out of their nose at lunch, or which teacher snores the loudest when they fall asleep in class.

Becky's text that night was the best. It made me realize that as bad as today had been, it wasn't a total waste.

Becky: They're making this short kid and this freakishly tall girl and a fat kid be in something called Safety Patrol

Becky now knows I exist!

# CHAPTER 7

The next day I got to school early and went to the library. I like to hide there until class starts. It's the last place Roy would hang out.

Plus, I like books. This morning I was reading *Huckleberry Finn*. It's really good—even though it was written a million years ago. It's about this kid, Huck, who runs away with a slave named Jim. They float down the Mississippi River. Lots of cool stuff happens.

Huck and Jim are cooler than anyone I know. They look out for each other. Sometimes, I wish I had someone like Jim to look out for me. Like when I'm sitting in the library, and I think

NICK FINN

I'm alone. A friend like Jim could warn me that a mutant troll bully is about to suck me into its gravitational field.

Roy caught me completely by surprise: No sound. No smell. I guess he ran out of body spray.

I looked up to find him staring right at me. His eyes were like two tiny black holes sucking in everything in their gaze.

I closed my eyes. When I opened them again, I was back in my locker.

It was just as well. Being stuffed in my locker meant I was safe from Dr. Daniels. And from Safety Patrol. And, I suddenly realized, safe from trying and failing to do pull-ups in gym.

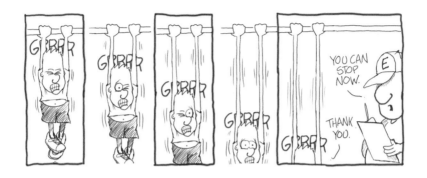

At first I thought Roy had done me a favor, but then I remembered that if I'm late for class one more time I'll get DETENTION!

And I wouldn't be alone. Detention is Roy's after-school home away from home.

I had to get out of my locker. And to make matters worse, my butt was tingling all the way down to my toes. I had a full-on case of zombie butt. There was no way I was getting out without some help.

I couldn't yell. I'd just end up in the office again and still be late to class. I needed to text a friend to come rescue me. That's when I realized . . .

I didn't have any friends.

But I did have those two phone numbers Dr. Daniels made me get from my Safety Patrol team members.

Karl would probably help, but then he'd want to hang out, and pretty soon we'd both be dragging matching suitcase backpacks down the hall.

But how could I text Molly? I barely knew her. She wasn't going to help me. Unless . . . unless I helped her.

Nick: I need u.

Molly: Who r u?

Nick: Nick!! Dr. D's office? I'm stuck in my locker

Molly: ?

Nick: in my locker!

Molly: ???

Nick: A MUTANT TROLL BULLY STUFFED ME IN!!!!

Molly: U don't have 2 yell

Nick: Plez get me out

Molly: Get urself out

Nick: I HAVE ZOMBIE BUTT!!

Molly: U should have that looked at

Nick: MY LEGS ARE ASLEEP!! Get me out, and I'll tell u how we can stay out of Safety Patrol. First floor. # 187. Hurry!

Molly: U R pathetic.

Nick: Hello? r u coming?

Nick: Hello?

# CHAPTER 8

Just when I was starting to think Molly wasn't going to come and I'd begun to wonder if I'd have to have my butt amputated, my locker door opened. "Great! Thanks," I said. "Help me out of here."

Molly put her hand up. "Not before you tell me how we're going to get out of Safety Patrol."

I told her.

She wasn't impressed. "Your plan is that we forge a doctor's note that says we're allergic to

safety?"

"I once got the nurse to excuse me from gym for being allergic to sweat," I argued.

"You made me come down here for *that*? You're pathetic! I'm leaving you in there!" she yelled as she started to shut the locker door on me.

"Please!" I begged. "I can't get detention! Just get me out of here, and I swear I'll come up with a better plan."

Molly just stared at me. Then she rolled her eyes, turned around, and said, "Hop on."

*Hop on?* I wasn't going to let a girl give me a piggyback ride. "No way," I said. I mean, how much humiliation can I take?

"Fine. Be late for class."

I guess I can take a lot of humiliation. Which is a good thing, because once I was on her back I suddenly saw the world in a whole new way.

I could see EVERYTHING! I could see the

entire school. I could see every teacher, every student, and every clique. I could see the OMGs.

And the Emogoths.

And the Unsociables.

And . . . trouble. We saw Roy and his pals,
The Future Inmates of America.

Roy and the FIA had Emily Dickinson Middle
School's only single-member clique in their
sights. That's when we stopped and hid.

We were just about to make a tiptoe escape, when

I got a call from . . . KARL?

He asked, "Wanna hang out?"

"NOW?" I whispered a bit too loudly.

Roy and the FIA spotted us. Molly and I took off down the hall. We rounded a corner into a crowd of students. I got down on my hands and knees and yanked Molly down with me. We crawled into an empty classroom and hid behind a projector. We waited. Nothing happened for a minute or so. We thought we were safe. But we weren't.

That's when things went from bad to worse . . . to weird.

We were saved by the fire alarm. Normally, we're all in class for fire drills, and everyone lines up single file to follow a teacher outside. But no one was in class yet. So no one knew where to go.

Except for Safety Patrolman Karl.

Karl did what he was trained to do: he pointed to the exits. This was his first mistake.

His second mistake was thinking his Safety Patrol belt was a real belt. Because somehow, by the time we all got outside, Karl had gotten separated from his pants.

Karl's third mistake was wearing NanoNerd underwear.

And his fourth and final mistake was letting Roy find his pants before he did.

Everyone laughed and pointed as Roy made Karl jump for his pants.

That's when something inside me snapped. I thought someone should do something. Then, just as I decided that that someone should be me, Molly decided it should be her.

Molly and I both rushed up to Roy at the same time. When I got there, I was so pumped, I said something really dumb:

WE'RE THE SAFETY PATROL, AND YOU BETTER NOT MESS WITH US OR ELSE!

Molly whispered to me, "Or else what?"

"I haven't thought that far ahead," I whispered back.

Karl said, "I don't think this is helping."

That's when Roy let go of Karl's pants and went after me.

Roy grabbed my leg and lifted me upside down. "This doesn't look very safe to me, Safety Patrol Boy!" he laughed.

As I was hanging there, I heard someone yell something from behind us. It didn't sound like a kid. But it didn't sound like an adult either. I turned around to see who it was, but there was no one there.

A kid yelled, "What?"

The same strange voice yelled again. I couldn't make it out. A different kid asked, "Bring what? Bring the crazy?"

And I thought, *Right. Like that's going to work.*

But when Roy threatened to bust me like a piñata, I decided crazy was worth a try.

So I started barking like a seal and flapping my arms like a chicken.

Roy's eyes got real wide. He started to look confused. And maybe a little . . . scared?

And then he released me.

It was working. I decided to push it up a notch. I . . .

Roy was backing off, but not fast enough. I was just about to run out of crazy when Molly joined in.

It took Karl a little longer to catch on. But once he got going, he brought his own "special" kind of crazy.

After Karl busted his ballet move, Roy just stood there. He looked to the crowd of kids for help. But everyone just stared back in silence. Roy was alone. And maybe, for the first time, a little afraid.

Then . . . he just took off.

That's when the weirdest part of all happened. The crowd started to cheer. And for the very first time, they cheered *with* us, and not *against* us.

Molly, Karl, and I all looked at each other.

Mr. Dupree was right: bringing the crazy really worked. We felt good. Really, really good.

It lasted about twelve seconds.

Still, it was twelve seconds I wouldn't give back.

As we all started filing back into the school, I spotted Mr. Dupree and yelled, "Thanks for reminding me to bring the crazy."

Mr. Dupree shook his head. "I just walked out here."

"If it wasn't you, then who was it?" I said.

Mr. Dupree eyes got really wide. "Emmmily . . ." He trembled.

Karl gasped. "She exists!"

Mr. Dupree nodded. "And she's been busy, because I think she set the fire alarm off, too."

WHOA.

SHE'S EVERYWHERE.

I rolled my eyes as Molly said, "He's just messing with you, Karl. There's no such thing as Emily."

"That voice was probably just someone who heard Mr. Dupree bring the crazy in the hallway yesterday," I said. "And the office just got the time wrong on a fire drill."

"Wait? What happened yesterday?" asked Molly.

"It doesn't matter," I said. "The important thing is that after today, I won't ever get stuffed in a locker again."

Mr. Dupree smiled. "Expectation is the root of all heartache."

Molly and Karl looked confused. I shook my head. "Don't ask."

Mr. Dupree said, "Tomorrow morning. Seven thirty. In the basement."

"Why? What's happening then?" I asked.

THE FIRST MEETING OF THE SAFETY PATROL, OF COURSE.

# CHAPTER 9

The next morning, Molly, Karl, and I stood in the school basement.

Alone.

Mr. Dupree was nowhere to be found in the mess of janitorial supplies and school junk from dinosaur days when they watched movies by hand.

We were just about to leave when we heard a voice say, "Welcome to Safety Patrol."

We looked up and found Mr. Dupree sitting on a bucket—like he'd been there the whole time. He was wearing a weird-looking hat. He looked serious. Which was hard to do in that hat.

Karl raised his hand. "Can I be captain?"

"Let's figure what you want to accomplish first," said Mr. Dupree. "What's your goal?"

We looked at one another, then did what we always do when we don't know what'll happen if we give the wrong answer: we shrugged.

Mr. Dupree shook his head. "First rule of Safety Patrol: no shrugging!"

That seemed extreme.

"Tell me, *why* are you here?" he said.

Karl raised his hand again. "I thought there'd be doughnuts."

"We want to make the school safe from bullies!" interrupted Molly.

I looked at Molly and said, "We do?"

"Yesterday, everyone was on our side. It was the first time I felt like I fit in," said Molly. "Lik I was popular. Bullies don't pick on popular kids."

I said, "So?"

"If everyone fits in, no one will get bullied! We need to help everyone fit in!"

"Even Karl?" I asked.

WERE KIDS SMALLER IN THE OLDEN DAYS?

Molly nodded. "Even Karl."

As we talked, Mr. Dupree smiled that grown-up smile that should come with its own thought balloon.

Mr. Dupree said, "You won a point. You didn't win the match. And you don't win the match by making friends. You win by taking from the other side the thing they're trying to take from you."

KIDS' HEADS ARE FILLED WITH GUM.

"Their pants." Karl nodded.

Mr. Dupree shook his head. "Have you ever heard the story about the man in India who went to live in the jungle with the tigers?"

We all shook our heads no.

"The man thought all creatures could live together in harmony. He believed that he could live with tigers. He thought they would accept him as one of their own. He lived and played among them for weeks."

Karl smiled. "Nice tigers."

"One day, the man brought one of the tigers a banana to eat. The tiger looked at the banana and then at the man. You know what happened next?"

Karl raised his hand. "The tiger gave him a hug?"

"The tiger ate him."

Karl looked at his shoes. "I don't like this story."

Mr. Dupree leaned forward and whispered, "Tigers don't fit in. They don't have to. Be the tiger, not the stupid man."

Molly and Karl were a little freaked out, but I had heard Mr. Dupree's stories before.

"That sounds like another one of your 'lies that tell the truth,'" I said.

Molly said, "Wait. How can a lie tell the truth?"

"Exactly." I nodded. I turned to Mr. Dupree and said, "How *can* a lie tell the truth?"

He smiled. "Patience. Though she be a tired mare, yet she will plod."

I had no idea what that meant. I turned to Molly, but she just shrugged. And Karl was . . . well . . . you know . . .

By the time Molly and I pried Karl out of that desk, Mr. Dupree was gone. In his place on the mop bucket were two brand-new Safety Patrol badges.

Molly said, "We don't need badges."

Karl was disappointed. "We don't?"

Molly shook her head. "Mr. Dupree is wrong: we definitely need to fit in. Those badges will jus make us stick out. We can't help other kids fit in if we don't fit in."

"How are we going to help other kids fit in?" I asked.

"We get the popular kids to accept them or else—"

"We bring *more* crazy." I nodded.

"But what about the tigers?" asked Karl.

Molly turned to Karl. "There aren't any tigers, Karl!"

"You're sure?" asked Karl as he chewed on his fingernails. "I really don't want to get eaten."

"No one's going to eat you, Karl," I said.

I DUNNO...

I TASTE PRETTY GOOD.

I shook my head and thought, *Welcome to Safety Patrol.*

# CHAPTER 10

Tigers are not our friends.

Mr. Dupree was right. Molly was wrong. And what I got for trying to upset the natural order was another case of zombie butt.

What went wrong? What *didn't* go wrong?

Our plan was for each of us to help one unpopular kid fit in.

Karl picked Warren Pickles. Warren is the only kid in school who doesn't move away when Karl sits down for lunch.

Warren has a problem with personal space: he doesn't believe in it.

Karl's mission was to get Warren accepted by the Unsociables. Which sounds like it would be easy. Strange attracts stranger. Right? Wrong.

It turns out that even the socially lame have boundaries. Warren bulldozed right past those and made himself at home.

The result? The Unsociables hung Karl and Warren up by their shorts. It took a block and pulley and twenty minutes taking turns, but they did it.

While Karl waited for rescue, Molly tried to get the OMGs to embrace Emily Dickinson Middle School's resident wallflower, Alice Frektner. Molly figured the OMGs would leap at such a tempting makeover challenge. But they didn't leap. They just sort of stood there and stared.

The problem was that Alice is what Memaw would call "plain." As in, plain hard to see. She's just sort of not there. Which made her kind of difficult to introduce.

The OMGs thought Molly was crazy. And not "bring the crazy" crazy. More like "get back, we don't want to catch your crazy" kind of crazy.

My mission was the hardest. And the most dangerous. I decided I was going to go epic or go home.

I decided to recruit Roy to the human race.

What I imagined would happen is I'd walk up to Roy and be all . . .

What actually happened was I walked up to him and said, "Dude!"

Roy immediately turned to me, and for just a

second, he looked just a little scared.

And then he didn't.

I said, "We're cool, right?"

As soon as I said *right*, I knew nothing was right. Roy's black-hole eyes narrowed. He growled. Then snarled. And I think he snorted once or twice.

I panicked.

I brought the crazy.

Nothing happened. Roy just sat there. Mr. Dupree never mentioned there was an expiration date on bringing the crazy.

The entire cafetorium was watching. I quickly looked around, searching for help—but there wasn't any.

When I turned back, I came face to face with Roy's gut. I leaned back and slowly looked up. . . .

You don't want Jell-O-Meat dumped on you. Jell-O-Meat stains. Jell-O-Meat stains skin. Like a tattoo. Only light-years less cool.

I screamed. I ducked. I dove. I ran.

And hid.

Like I said, Roy can't stuff me in my locker if I'm already in it. It's not so bad.

Except for the zombie butt.

# CHAPTER 11

After school, Molly, Karl, and I met near the buses. Molly and I agreed we were done with Safety Patrol. Karl wasn't so sure. On the one hand, fire exits don't point out themselves; but on the other hand, due to constant wedgies, he was running out of underwear.

We were right back where we started. Only worse. It was like we had never stood up to Roy, and the other kids had never cheered, and we were never popular for a whole twelve seconds.

Now, *everyone* knew who we were. Everyone knew who *I* was.

I was famous.

Not movie-star famous. More like that-kid-in-the-YouTube-video-who-gets-his-head-stuck-in-a-mailbox kind of famous. Everyone knows you.

No one wants to be anywhere near you.

Just like on the bus that day.

I sat there watching the kids in front whisper to one another and look back at me, and I thought of something Mom told me right after she and Dad split up:

That made feel better until I looked out the window and saw Roy and Becky. Together. AGAIN!

And . . . she was touching him! On the *ARM!*
*ON PURPOSE!*

She can't do that! It's not allowed! It's
unnatural! Mutant Troll Bully–human touching
is strictly forbidden according to Rule 6 in the
Top 10 Rules for When I Run the Universe:

10. ALL LOCKERS PADDED
9. ALL SHORT KIDS: FREE PIZZA
8. NANONERD'S NANOSUIT AVAILABLE IN BOY'S SMALL
7. ALL JELL-O MEAT DUMPED IN TOXIC LAND FILL
6. NO HUMAN TO MUTANT TOUCHING EVER
5. ALL PEER MEDIATION GROUPS OUTLAWED
4. ALL CATS GET DOG PERSONALITY TRANSPLANTS
3. FREE YOGA FOR ALL GRANDMAS
2. NURSES WORSHIPPED LIKE GODS
1. FREE MAC-N-CHEESE FOR EVERYONE

I turned away from the window, sank down in
my seat, and stared at my shoes. "'Nothing will
come of nothing,'" said a voice from outside the bus.

I looked out the window again. Mr. Dupree
was staring up at me. I said, "You just make this
stuff up, don't you?"

"You're not the first person in the history of
the world to have a tough day."

I stared straight ahead.

"You ever hear about the abominable snow
goat?"

I rolled my eyes. "There's no such thing."

"Maybe there is. Maybe there isn't," he said. "No one's ever really seen one up close. Talk about having a tough day. They live at twenty thousand feet in the snow and ice of the Himalayas, where there's only enough oxygen for one abominable snow goat every ten miles."

He said, "It would be easy for them to live down with the regular goats where there's plenty of air to breathe and plenty of goats to breathe it with."

I ignored him as the bus started.

"You know why they don't go live with the other goats?"

The bus started to move.

Mr. Dupree smiled. "Because then they wouldn't have a chance to be on top of the world."

# CHAPTER 12

**W**hen I got home, I wasn't thinking about Mr. Dupree's snow goats. All I could think about was how Becky may be scarred for life after touching Roy's Mutant Troll acid oozing skin and how I couldn't wait to get to my room and start text-torturing Roy.

I made a beeline for Memaw's phone, but quickly realized there was no way I was going to get it anytime soon.

YOU'RE GETTING SLEEPY...

When you see your grandma hypnotizing a dog, you stop. "Why are you hypnotizing Janice?"

"So she'll stop farting," Memaw said.

Janice looked at me like she wanted to say:

I AM A DOG.
I FART.
IT'S WHAT I DO.

Before I could rescue Janice, Memaw started reading a book on her lap. "'Once the subject is relaxed they will become open to any suggestion.'"

Memaw looked at Janice. "When I snap my fingers you will stop farting."

Janice farted.

"I must be doing something wrong," she said as she grabbed her can of deodorizer and started spraying.

TOOT!

SNAP

"I don't think you can hypnotize dogs," I said.

"Okay, then I'll hypnotize you."

"I don't have a farting problem."

"I'm sure we can think of something you need to improve on."

You can run from Memaw. But you can't hide. She'll just hunt you down to cut your hair with a vacuum cleaner or force you to be her yoga assistant.

"I've got it!" said Memaw. "You need to eat more beets!"

"No one eats beets," I whined.

"They build strong spleens."

"Memaw, please!"

"'Nothing will come of nothing.'"

"What did you say?"

"It's Shakespeare. It means if we don't try, we can't succeed. Now, sit down and let me hypnotize you."

"Who's Shakespeare?"

Memaw looked at me like I just spit in her oatmeal, then proceeded to tell me more than I ever wanted to know about some old dude who wrote a bunch of plays a million years ago.

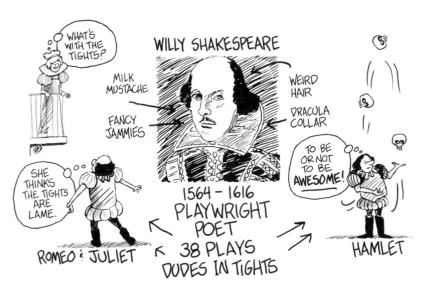

As Memaw lectured, I pretty much lost track of what year it was. Before I could recover, she started to swing her pill container in front of me whispering,

She snapped her fingers. Janice farted. Then peed on the rug.

Memaw immediately turned to me and said, "Your mother doesn't need to know about this."

I smiled. "Deal."

While Memaw went to the kitchen to get some sort of cleanser that kills alien parasites, I snatched her cell phone and ran upstairs to my room, texting Roy on the way.

Max: U seen Ty O'rea?
Roy: Who's Ty O'rea?
Max: U R Ty O'rea!

Long pause. Then:

Roy: I'm going 2 strangle the snot out a U!!!!
Max: HAHAHAHAHAHAHAHAHAHA

Max is a lot funnier than I am. I mean, I'm funnier as Max than I am as me.

After I messed with Roy for a while, Max got a text from Becky.

Becky: u c that short safety patrol kid in the cafetorium?
Max: 1 who almost got a jell-o-meat tat?
Becky: Yeah, he tried 2 make friends w/ Roy

Max: 2 stupid

Becky: 2 brave

I thought, "Wait? What? She thinks I'm brave?"

Becky: r we going 2 meet?

Max: short kid?

Becky: No. u, stupid. after school tomorrow?

Max: Cant. Skydiving practice

Becky: ???

Max: L8R gator

Sure, the skydiving thing was lame. But I had a bigger problem: could I really afford to quit Safety Patrol? I decided to work it out with a logic tree.

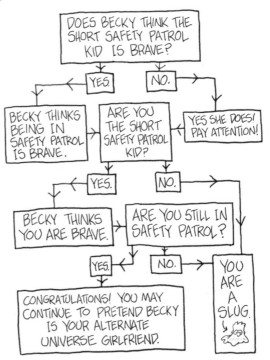

It was clear what I had to do. I erased the messages on Memaw's phone, picked up my own phone, and immediately texted Molly and Karl:

Nick: Meet me in the basement before school tmrrw

Molly: What? Why? We're not in Safety Patrol anymore

Nick: Just do it. I'll explain

Karl: This is my first text. I'm so excited!

Karl: Guys?

Karl: Guys?

Karl: What am I doing wrong?

Karl: Guys?

# CHAPTER 13

The next morning, I stood across from Karl and The Stare Master in the school basement and told them we shouldn't quit Safety Patrol.

They weren't very receptive.

"You want us to keep going after yesterday!" yelled Molly.

Karl rubbed his butt. "It still chafes!"

I couldn't tell them the truth. I couldn't tell them my alternate universe girlfriend thought what I did the day before with Roy was brave.

So I told them, "We need to stay in Safety Patrol because nothing equals something. I mean something plus nothing equals nothing. No, that's not right, it's nothing minus something times nothing equals something."

*I WAS NEVER GOOD AT MATH.*

93

"Safety Patrol? That is SO lame!"

We turned around. Roy stood at the top of the stairs. He laughed. "What are you? Some sort of Super Secret Freak Force?"

In case I haven't mentioned it, Molly really hates being called a freak. She skips the Stare Master stage and transforms straight into the Were-Molly.

Karl said, "You can't be down here."

Roy leaned over Karl and said, "Who's going to stop me?"

"We're going to stop you!" said Molly, as she launched a plunger directly at Roy's head.

Roy looked up. He wasn't happy. "Who DID that?!"

Roy furiously tugged at the plunger, but it wouldn't budge. He finally gave up, lowered his head, and charged.

Just as the lights went out.

"What's going on?"

The lights came back on. We looked up and saw Mr. Dupree glaring at us from the top of the stairs.

Mr. Dupree quickly came down the stairs and helped Roy up (with the plunger still attached to his head).

I smiled. "You can keep the hat."

As Roy was leaving, I whispered to Molly, "I guess you're back."

"Shut up," said Molly.

Mr. Dupree said, "Who was that kid?"

We all shrugged.

Mr. Dupree shook his head. "What did I say was the first rule of Safety Patrol?

We all looked down and said, "No shrugging."

"When I said, 'Be the tiger and not the stupid man,' I meant be smarter, not stronger. You want to control your opponent. And you can't do that without controlling yourself."

Karl raised his hand. "I can go three hours without blinking."

Mr. Dupree ignored Karl. "And the first step to controlling yourself is to know yourself. To know your strengths *and* your weaknesses."

Karl raised his hand again. "I have a shy bladder!" Then, realizing his mistake, he added, "Please don't tell anyone."

Mr. Dupree went on. "To know what you know

and what you don't know, and especially what you don't know that you don't know."

I thought, I'm pretty sure I know that I don't know what he's talking about.

"You start by gathering intelligence," said Mr. Dupree.

Mr. Dupree shook his head. "Leave the seventh graders alone, Karl."

Mr. Dupree started to leave. "Tomorrow we'll start learning the basics of intelligence gathering: disguises, surveillance, and secure communications."

After Mr. Dupree left, I turned to Molly. "He knows it's Roy we're after."

"How?" asked Molly.

"The lights! He had to have turned them off just as Roy charged," I said. "And I think he also pulled the alarm, and somehow was the voice from the soccer field. I think he's helping us."

"How do you know it wasn't Emily?" said Karl.

"Because Emily doesn't exist!" I said.

Karl said, "Well, maybe if you believed in her."

Molly shook her head. "But he asked us who Roy was. Maybe he really doesn't know?"

"He knows," I said. "He can't help us if he knows we know he knows it's Roy."

"I'm confused," said Karl.

"He'd have to turn Roy in, right?" I said.

Molly nodded. "And then Roy would go even harder after us."

"Mr. Dupree is cool. He's on our side," I said.

Karl started clapping as he searched around the basement.

"Karl, what are you doing?" I asked.

IT WORKED FOR TINKER BELL.

CLAP CLAP

That night, while Memaw was sleeping through *The Deep Fat Fry Guy* on Eat Network . . .

. . . Max was upstairs texting Roy:

DAT LOBSTER AIN'T SCREAMIN'. HE SAYIN' **WEEEEE!**

AYEEEE!

Max: Hey Roy, what r worst 4 years in a bully's life?

Roy: u text me again, I'll . . .

Max: 3rd grade! Hahahahahaha!!!

Roy: u r going 2 b sorry when I figure out who u r.

Max: going 2 be hard with that fly buzzing in ur head. What's his name? Space Invader? Roy:

U r DEAD!!!

Max: HAHAHAHAHAHAHAHAHA!!!

Roy really cheers me up sometimes. He has the gift.

Just as I started to text Roy again, there was a knock on the door. "Nick, have you seen my phone?" asked Memaw.

"No," I lied. "Did you check the recliner?"

Memaw nodded. "I don't understand technology. Does it have an invisible mode?"

I shook my head. "If I find it, I'll let you know."

"I need it to text my vote against deep-fried lobster. Can you imagine such a thing?"

I shook my head again.

"What's that buzzing?" asked Memaw.

"What buzzing?" I lied again. "I don't hear anything."

Memaw pointed to my bed. "It came from . . ."

"Do you still hear it?" I asked.

"No. It stopped."

I could hear Mom down the hall, yelling, "What's going on?"

"I heard buzzing," said Memaw.

Mom came to door. She looked at me.

"I didn't hear anything," I said.

Mom looked at Memaw. Memaw rolled her eyes and said, "Go ahead."

Then Mom did her nurse thing.

FOLLOW MY FINGER.

I'D RATHER PULL YOUR FINGER.

"You're fine," said Mom

"Of course I'm fine!" said Memaw, turning to me. "It's probably that fly in my head. What's his name?"

"Space Invader." I smiled.

Memaw walked off down the hall, banging her

hand against her head like when you're trying to get water out of your ears.

Mom looked at me. "You're sure you didn't hear anything?"

"Jeez, Mom, no!" I lied again.

That was my third lie in five minutes. I felt bad. I wished she would just leave.

She looked at me, sighed, and said, "I'm sorry. I guess I just don't want to think Memaw's getting old."

Then she walked over and gave me a hug.

She smiled, turned, and left, shutting the door behind her.

Like a cell door. In a dungeon. Like the one in the Zogex Quadrant on the Planet Frodark,

where the Giant Sand Squid of Lagslag imprisoned NanoNerd for life.

Memaw's phone buzzed again. I dove under the bed and silenced the buzzer.

It was a text from Becky:

Becky: Therz no skydiving club.

Busted! I had to think fast.

Max: Sorry. Didn't want u to think I was loser 4 being in Chess Club.
Becky: Chess iz cool. Meet tmrrw?
Max: Can't. We've got a match with Wendell Willkie.
Becky: Soon, ok?
Max: Soon.

# CHAPTER 15

You can't lie just once.

Lies have a way of multiplying. They can't stand on their own. Each lie leads to bigger lies that lead to even bigger lies until it looks something like this:

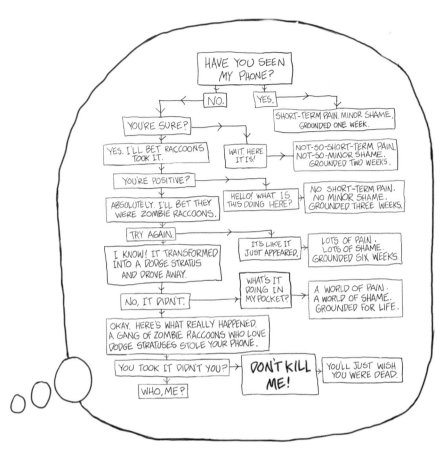

That's a lot of lies.

One day, I might have to tell the truth.

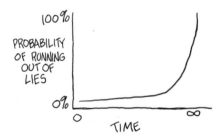

One day.

# CHAPTER 16

Over the next week, Molly, Karl, and I met before and after school with Mr. Dupree and got a crash course in intelligence gathering (no seventh graders were harmed in this process).

First up: disguises.

Mr. Dupree gave us some stage makeup and a box of old clothes to practice with.

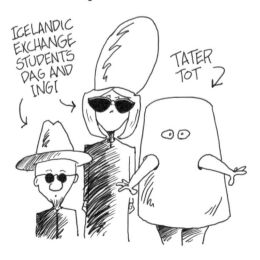

ICELANDIC EXCHANGE STUDENTS DAG AND INGI

TATER TOT

He said, "The trick is to alter your appearance just enough to make you look different without looking stupid."

We got it half right.

Next up: surveillance.

Surveillance means watching people without their knowing you're watching them . . .

. . . following people without their knowing you're following them . . .

CHUNKA
CHUNKA
CHUNKA

. . . and listening to people without their knowing you're listening to them.

Mr. Dupree told us surveillance is an art. He didn't say anything about coloring within the lines.

The last intelligence-gathering skill was secure communication.

Stuff like coded messages.

And relaying messages with animals.

Meanwhile, Roy's reign of terror didn't take a break just because we were learning to be spies. Wedgies, insults, and zombie butt continued just like before.

We couldn't wait to take Roy down. Sure, we stumbled a bit in training, but when we met after the week was up we thought we had intelligence-gathering wired.

We were wrong.

Mr. Dupree said, "Good start. Another few weeks, and you'll be ready."

"A few weeks!" I cried.

Mr. Dupree smiled and said, "'Thou know'st the first time that we smell the air we wawl and cry.'"

I'd had it with those stupid quotes of his. I lost it:

Karl raised his hand. "Poop smells bad."

I pleaded with Mr. Dupree. "Pleazzzzzzze!"

Mr. Dupree shook his head. "A little information is a dangerous thing. And you can't even gather that much yet. We'll practice some more on Monday."

# CHAPTER 17

As Molly, Karl, and I walked out of school, I said, "I really thought Mr. Dupree was helping us."

"It's not fair," added Molly.

"I really am out of underwear," said Karl.

I heard laughing behind us. I turned around to see Becky and Roy walking out of school together. I stopped and stared as they continued to totally ruin my life.

"Why are you staring like that? Is it that girl?" asked Molly.

"She's not important. We need to go after Roy *now*."

Molly said, "You know, it didn't go so well when we ignored Mr. Dupree the last time."

Behind us Roy yelled:

I smiled. "Good. Let's meet at my house on Saturday to plan."

"A playdate?" clapped Karl.

Molly and I glared at Karl, then started walking. We tried to ignore him . . .

. . . but Karl is really, really hard to ignore.

# CHAPTER 18

On Saturday Molly and Karl came over and we started planning Operation: Bully Bait.

Bully Bait was Molly's idea. She and Karl nixed my name: Operation: Reduce Roy to a Quivering Mass of Goo.

We were alone in the house. Mom was at work, and Memaw was at her yoga class.

I stood in front of a portable chalkboard. "Let's start by thinking of ways to take down Roy."

Molly wondered if maybe we should start by gathering intelligence. I was

# WANTED

FOR
BULLYING, JERKINESS, MEANNESS, ALL AROUND MUTANT TROLLNESS
AND BUTT BREATH

pretty sure feeding him to giant sand fleas would be quicker, but I was willing to listen.

Molly said, "The more we know about Roy, the easier it'll be to control him."

Karl raised his hand. "Let's bug him!"

I looked at Molly. "I think we already bug him enough."

"No!" said Karl as he reached into his backpack and pulled out a baby monitor. "I mean listen in on him."

"Why do you have a baby monitor, Karl?" I asked.

"I'm fixing it. My parakeet spilled his water on it," Karl explained.

"It was in his cage?" asked Molly.

"In case he needs anything. You know, like food, a foot rub, or maybe a different hat to go with his sailor outfit.

Molly and I looked at each other. I said,

"Maybe he spilled water on it because he wants to be alone."

Karl looked really confused. "Why would he want that?"

Molly said, "Let's get back to Roy."

Karl continued, "Roy's backpack is the same as Molly's. We sew the monitor into the lining and listen in with the receiver. All I have to do is swap backpacks with Roy."

Molly and I just stared at Karl. It was actually a good plan. Which was odd, since it came from Karl.

Molly said, "I'll do the swap."

"Why can't I do the swap?" said Karl.

"You came up with the plan," I offered.

"You guys aren't ever going to let me do anything, are you?" said Karl.

"Nick! Nick! How do I send a text? Nick?!" said Memaw from the doorway.

That was harsh. Harsh, but true.

I introduced Molly and Karl. I told Memaw we were helping Karl with his project for the upcoming science fair.

"My project is 'Will It Twist?'" said Karl. "I'm testing the torsional twist strength of fruits, vegetables, toys . . ."

Memaw looked concerned. "You're going to twist things until they come apart?"

Karl nodded eagerly.

I interrupted. "You said you needed to send a text?"

Memaw dug her phone out of her purse. "I got a message from some jerk who wants to pound me into Jell-O-Meat."

Molly said, "Jell-O-Meat?"

"If it happens again, I'm going to take him out," said Memaw.

I HAVE A PINK BELT IN YOGA!

I took the phone from Memaw and said, "You don't need to text him back. I'll just block his number." I erased the message, blocked Roy, and handed the phone back to Memaw. "All fixed."

Memaw smiled at Molly and Karl, closed the door, and walked off down the hall mumbling to herself, "I'll do it. I'll bring the pain."

Molly looked at me. "Why is Roy texting your grandmother?"

"Roy?" I said. "What makes you think it's Roy? It could be anybody that—"

The Stare Master stared me down.

"Okay, it's Roy," I admitted.

"Roy bullies grandmothers?" said Karl. "I gotta warn mine."

I didn't see a way to lie my way out of this. But I certainly couldn't tell the whole truth. I said, "I might have used Memaw's phone to text Roy a few times."

Molly shook her head. "You texted Roy as your grandmother?"

"I couldn't use my own phone," I said. "He'd know who I was. And my texts haven't exactly been nice." Molly stared me down again. "Okay, they've been pretty mean. Enough to upset him. A lot."

Molly and Karl traded a look. I continued, "It's no big deal and it's nothing like what he does to us. It's just a tiny little way to, you know, get even."

Molly looked at me for long moment. She nodded. "I think it's awesome."

"Me too," said Karl.

"You do?"

Molly smiled. "What sort of stuff did you text him?"

I grinned. "Knock knock."

"Who's there?" asked Karl.

"Ida."

"Ida Who?"

"Ida your face, you're scaring babies."

# CHAPTER 19

Monday morning we launched Operation Bully Bait with me getting stuffed in my locker again. This time on purpose.

I risked more zombie butt so we could swap backpacks with Roy. I'm proud to say it takes two hands to stuff me in my locker.

SHOVE!

After the switch, we stashed the baby monitor receiver along with a digital recorder in my locker. We wrapped them both in a bunch of gym clothes to dampen the sound. We didn't want some sixth grader freaking out because he thought Emily was hanging out in his locker.

Then we met with Mr. Dupree for more intelligence-gathering practice. We didn't want him to suspect we'd gone after Roy on our own, so we needed him to think we were still hopeless.

SCANDINAVIAN EXCHANGE STUDENTS HERLUF AND ASTRID

BLURT

DODGEBALL

Which we were getting pretty good at.

After school, we grabbed the baby monitor and recorder and ran to the bleachers behind the soccer field to listen to Roy's day.

We turned on the recorder. The first thing

we heard was Becky saying, "Same time? Same place?" followed by Roy saying, "Yeah, see you after school."

"I knew you liked her!" said Molly as she punched me in the arm. "We're here to deal with Roy, not rescue your stupid girlfriend. Got it?"

"Got it," I said. I noticed Karl with a goofy grin on his face. "What is it, Karl?"

"You've got a girlfriend," he said. "And Molly has a . . . a . . ."

"A mission," said Molly.

Karl continued, "And I have my parakeet, my sea monkeys . . ."

That's when Karl lunged.

Then he let go and we looked at one another.
I said, "Let's please never do that again." Molly
nodded. Karl just grinned and said, "We'll see."

I quickly turned the recorder back on. We
learned a lot about Roy. Most of it was stuff we
already knew like . . .

Roy is an accomplished motivational speaker.

Roy is well traveled and extremely sophisticated.

There was also stuff we didn't know. Like, he doesn't read very well.

He mixes up his numbers and letters.

And he's really, really seriously afraid of losing something really, really seriously important to him.

I turned the recorder off. We all stared at our shoes.

Karl rubbed his stomach. "My tummy's all sideways."

"That was way more than I needed to know," added Molly.

I said, "Mr. Dupree was right. A little information is a dangerous thing."

Roy had managed to do the impossible. He had us all feeling sorry for him.

Molly turned the recorder back on.

Then quickly turned it off again.

Karl shook his head. "I tied my shoes in a triple knot once and had to throw them away."

Molly said, "Who's Max?"

That's when I realized that as tough as Roy might have it, it was Max who really needed our help.

I said, "Max is a dork. And what are we?"

Molly and Karl stared at me.

"We're the Dork Defenders!" I said.

"Dork Defenders," Molly repeated.

"Whatever," I said. "The point is, who cares if Roy can't read? We have to stop him! We have to help Max!"

Molly nodded and turned the recorder back on.

Roy continued, "Then I'm going to cover him in tuna and throw him in the Cat Dumpster

behind the Stop-N-Snarf."

Molly turned the recorder off again as Karl's eyes went wide. "Some of those cats can take down a cow," he said.

That was stupid, but I decided to go with it. "All the more reason to save Max from Roy," I said.

"But how?" asked Molly.

"Dr. Daniels's office," I said. "Roy said he was afraid of losing something. If we could find out what it is, we could . . ."

"We could what?" said Molly.

"If we took it, maybe he'd stop being a bully to get it back."

"But we don't even know what it is," said Molly.

"Dr. Daniels knows," I said. "And if she knows . . ."

Molly nodded. "It's in his permanent record!"

"They're not really permanent, are they?" asked Karl.

I said, "It's settled then. We're going to break into Dr. Daniels's office and get Roy's record."

Karl looked worried. "I mean, some day they'll just throw those records away, right?"

"And I know just how we can get in without anyone finding out," I added

"How?" asked Molly.

Karl started to panic. "If it's really

permanent, then when I grow up and invent the first backyard zero-gravity bouncy castle, everyone will know . . ."

Too late.

# CHAPTER 20

I knew how to break into Dr. Daniels's office because I'd done it before. I broke in once to swap out her annoying therapy puppets with something more interesting to talk to on my frequent visits.

There's a heating duct on the wall behind her desk that leads to another duct inside the first-floor boys' bathroom. After school one day I crawled in, dropped down, and swapped therapy dolls.

My sessions with Dr. Daniels were so much more fun after that.

MR. GRUMPY PANTS

MR. MEGA MEGALOMANIAC (NANONERD #78: FLOSS OR DIE)

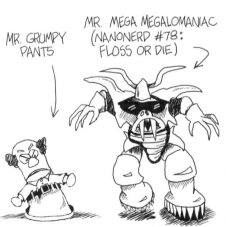

Operation: Bully Bait, Phase 1: Snatch-n-Snag to get Roy's permanent record was set for after school at the end of the week.

The plan was simple:

What could possibly go wrong?

# CHAPTER 21

The rest of that week we continued to meet with Mr. Dupree before school. We made sure that he noticed we were continuing to *not* make progress on our spy skills.

EASTER ISLAND EXCHANGE STUDENTS TAMATI AND POGISA

RHOMBUS

The night before the raid, as Memaw slept through her favorite reality show, *The Orphans,*

I snatched her phone, unblocked Roy's number, and went into Max mode:

> Max: Roy, u r so stupid u boil eggs in the microwave.
>
> Roy: u r so stupid, u dont know that u can.

"Wait. Really?" I said out loud.

I figured he was probably lying. After I

reblocked Roy's number, I decided it would be fun to find out.

Just as I started the microwave, Becky texted me.

Becky: Therz no chess club tmrrw. We're
    meeting after school.
Max: I got astronomy club.
Becky: In the afternoon?

Busted! Again!

Becky: Or we never meet.

Now I didn't know what to do. Max can't meet her. I have to stall. But how?

Then it hit me. I couldn't meet Becky as Max. But I could meet her as Max's best friend. I could meet her as . . .

ME! *

*THE BEST FRIEND
A MADE-UP FRIEND
EVER HAD!

Max: tmrrw after school by the sign. I'll be there.
Becky: C ya.

Then I thought, Isn't there something else tomorrow after school? I'm supposed to . . .
Uh-oh.

THE SNATCH -N- SNAG!

# CHAPTER 22

**I** had a plan. It was a good plan. No, it was a great plan. In the entire world history of plans, my plan was one of the best plans ever. Top 50, easy.

It was so simple. I would meet with Becky right after school for a few minutes, tell her Max was shy, and say he sent me, his best friend, instead. Then I'd join Molly and Karl for the break-in.

Best plan ever, right? Wrong.

"You're not Max," said Becky.

I shook my head no.

"You're the kid who brought the crazy. You and Roy have . . . issues."

I nodded.

"Why can't you talk? Are you sick?"

"Laryngitis?"

I nodded really fast.

Becky frowned. "I guess Max doesn't want to be seen with me."

No. That wasn't true! Max, I mean me, I mean WE do want to be seen with her.

Becky started to walk away. I couldn't let her go, but how could I explain? I had to do something, so I jumped in front of her and put my hands up. I looked at my hands and got an idea.

I could act it out. Like charades. Memaw and I play charades all the time.

I showed Becky the *sort of* real reason why
Max couldn't be there.

Becky smiled. "If Max is as nice as you, he has nothing to worry about."

She thought Max could be nice. She thought I was nice. And since there is no Max, that just leaves ME—with all the nice.

I started to think now would be a great time for Max to suddenly come down with a fatal disease that causes horrible face lesions.

Before Becky said good-bye, we exchanged phone numbers in case she needed me to get in touch with Max.

As Becky walked away, my phone buzzed. It was a text from Molly with a photo.

Molly: WHERE R YOU?! WE NEED U NOW!!!

138

**I** didn't mean to forget about Molly and Karl. It was an accident. I was distracted. I was just juggling too many things at once.

When I got to the duct above Dr. Daniels's office I was going to explain all this to Molly, bu she wasn't in the mood. She had her hands full.

"What happened?" I said.

"You were LATE! We went ahead without you."

"You couldn't wait five minutes?"

"Karl has a dance lesson."

Karl looked up at us. "Jazz/Tap."

"It's only four feet to the floor," I said. "Why didn't he just jump down?"

"He's afraid of heights!"

"That is not a height! That is a step!"

"He insisted on lowering himself with a rope. And then there was the spider."

"Spiders are evil," Karl pointed out.

I looked at Molly. "YOU'RE taller than the vent!"

"Karl wanted to do it."

Karl looked up. "You guys never let me do anything."

AND THIS IS WHY!

It took a few minutes to get Karl untangled. Just as he was about to crawl into the vent and let me take over, we heard a key slip into the office door.

"Karl, HIDE!" I whispered.

Dr. Daniels came through the door just as Karl dove behind a pile of therapy dolls in the corner.

Dr. Daniels looked around as though she'd heard something. At one point she stopped and stared at the doll pile. Molly and I held our breath. Dr. Daniels blinked a couple times and shook her head like she thought she was seeing things. Then she picked up a file from her desk and left, locking the door behind her.

Molly and I finally exhaled. I said, "Karl, get back up here, and I'll finish looking.

"No!" said both Molly and Karl.

"We'll finish it ourselves," said Molly. "You can go back and hang out with your *girlfriend*."

"I was not with—"

"You're lying!"

She was just like my mom. I thought, Is the whole mind-squish deal some sort of girl thing?

"How did you know I'm lying?" I asked.

"YOUR LIPS ARE MOVING!"

"Guys, I found Roy's permanent record," cried out Karl.

Molly and I looked down. Roy's permanent record was as thick as the big dictionary in the school  library. The one you only use to look up words you can't say out loud.

Molly whispered, "Start taking pictures of each page with your phone."

"That'll take forever," I said. "Just find Dr. Daniels's session notes. They're the yellow pages."

Molly interrupted, "No. The blue pages. The yellow pages are Incident Reports."

"No," I said. "The blue pages are Counselor Recommendation Forms."

"Those are purple!"

"Green!"

"I'm in her office more than you!

"Are you kidding? I LIVE here!"

Karl started reading from the file.  'Roy told me his greatest fear today. . . .'"

"That's it!" I cried.

"Go! Go! Go!" added Molly.

Karl aimed his phone at the file and started taking pictures. One page in, he stopped and looked up.

THE BATTERY WENT DEAD.

The Stare Master instantly trained her laser sights on me.

"Wait. How is the battery going dead my fault?" I protested.

"If you'd been on time and not getting all tater-brained with Becky, Karl's phone would still have worked."

"Fine. I'm a jerk. Are you happy?" I said as I dug my phone out of my pocket and started to hand it to Karl. "He can use mine."

Karl reached for my phone just as we heard someone singing outside the office door. It was Mr. Dupree. "'Lydia, oh Lydia, that encyclopedia. Lydia, the Queen of Tattoo!'"

"Now, Karl! Get out NOW!" I whispered. Molly and I reached down and grabbed Karl's arms and pulled him up.

We replaced the grate behind him just as Mr. Dupree unlocked the door and stepped into the office, pushing a mop bucket and whistling.

Then he suddenly stopped.

From inside the duct, we could hear Mr. Dupree walking toward us.

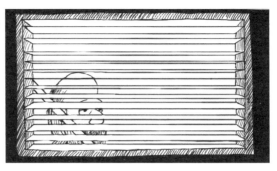

I could see Mr. Dupree look around the room. Then, just as he was going to look toward the duct . . .

It was the sprinklers outside. Mr. Dupree turned to the window, muttering, "Those aren't supposed to be on." He shook his head and walked toward the door, whistling as he went.

Nobody said anything as we started to crawl out. After a few seconds, I thought I'd break the tension.

# CHAPTER 24

**S**eriously, it wasn't that bad. We all got out safely. We got pictures of Roy's permanent record. Sure, Karl lost his pants, but that pretty much happens every day. Mission accomplished.

Molly didn't agree. Actually, she didn't say anything. When we got outside, she just scowled and walked off. After a few steps, she stopped and looked back at Karl and said, "Are you coming?"

Karl was confused.

Karl's no match for The Stare Master. He did as he was told.

I shrugged. She'll get over it, I thought. I don't have anything to apologize for. I'm glad I was late. If I hadn't been late, I wouldn't have found out Becky liked me, I mean Max. I mean—

"They don't look too happy," said Mr. Dupree from behind me.

I turned around. Mr. Dupree was pointing at Molly and Karl as he walked toward me, dragging a long hose with a spray nozzle attached. "Everything all right?" he asked.

"They're just tired of practicing," I lied. "They want to get started with Safety Patrol."

Mr. Dupree smiled. "'Sweet are the uses of adversity.'"

I stared at him. Once again, I had no idea what he was talking about.

"Did you know I was once a thumb-wrestling champion?" he asked.

I thought, How would I know that? How would anyone know that?

"I was fast, flexible, and strong. I once thumb pressed one hundred seventeen pounds.

You know how I got to be a thumb-wrestling champion?"

I rolled my eyes.

"By not thumb wrestling. My coach, the legendary Mo Gatsby, wouldn't let me. He made me do thumb circles, thumb-ups, and thumb squats until my thumb was about to fall off. But no wrestling."

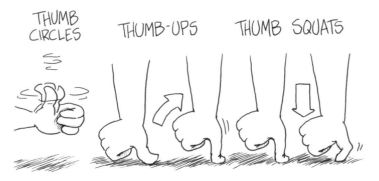

THUMB CIRCLES    THUMB-UPS    THUMB SQUATS

"He made me spar with his three-legged cat Otis over a piece of yarn. Otis was fast, but he wasn't faster than me."

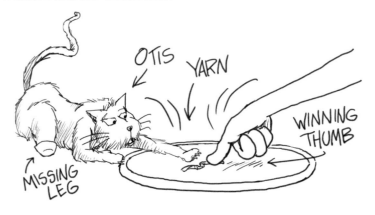

OTIS    YARN    WINNING THUMB    MISSING LEG

"Finally, after months, Coach Gatsby himself wrestled me. At first, he'd pin me in seconds but over time I got better, until one day when he had me in a Full-Nelson Nail-Biter, I reversed him with a Kobyashi Knuckle Drag and pinned him."

"So, he let you start competing?"

Mr. Dupree nodded. "I had to get out from under his thumb before I could put anyone under mine."

I groaned.

"It's true."

"Or another lie that tells the truth."

"Ah, so you understand now."

"I haven't understood a single thing you've said."

He smiled as he continued across the grass. "Don't worry. You'll figure it out."

As I watched Mr. Dupree fiddle with the spray nozzle, I wondered if he was acting *too* weird. Like he wants us to think he's weird, but he's really not. Like he's really trying to help us, after all. Maybe he knows what we're up to and he's just pretending to hold us back. Maybe he knew we were in Dr. Daniels's office the whole time

and somehow caused those sprinklers to go on to
cover our escape.

Maybe he really did do all that Emily stuff.
What if he's Emily? What if he's always been
Emily?

That's when the water suddenly came on and
blasted him in the face.

And then I thought, Maybe not.

# CHAPTER 25

$I$ got home to find Memaw practicing her hypnotism on Janice again.

She still wasn't having any luck. I was on my way to my room when Memaw said, "Hang on. I got another text from that rude person."

She showed me her phone:

Roy: I'm going to find u. When I do I'm gonna rip ur spleen out.

"Wait, I blocked his number," I said.

"I unblocked it."

"Why would you do that?"

"He could be annoying other old ladies. He needs to be stopped."

I tried to convince Memaw it was a wrong number. Besides, I seriously doubted that Roy knew what or where a spleen is.

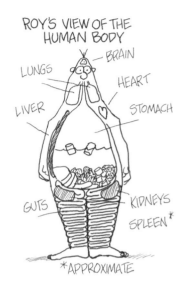

ROY'S VIEW OF THE HUMAN BODY

BRAIN
LUNGS
HEART
LIVER
STOMACH
GUTS
KIDNEYS
SPLEEN *
*APPROXIMATE

But it was too late. Memaw had already texted Roy back.

> Max: You are a bad person. You should be ashamed for threatening people's vital organs. It is MY spleen, not yours. How would you like it if I threatened to deprive you of your spleen? I thought so. Good day, sir!

"He'll think twice before he messes with me again," said Memaw.

If he can actually count to two, I thought.

# CHAPTER 26

Later that night, Memaw fell asleep watching *Cats with Hats* on the Pet Channel.

I snatched her phone again and ran upstairs. And right into Mom.

"What's the rush?"

"Gotta study. Big test tomorrow."

"In what?"

"Um . . . Social Studies."

"What's it on?"

Jeez, I thought, she's such a Mompire, always sucking me dry for useless information.

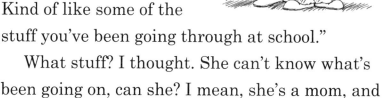

I said, "It's over stuff you have to go through to be part of a tribe."

"Oh. Initiation rites. Kind of like some of the stuff you've been going through at school."

What stuff? I thought. She can't know what's been going on, can she? I mean, she's a mom, and moms have superpowers, but still.

"The stuff you've been talking to Dr. Daniels about since school started?"

"Oh, right," I said. Whew. She didn't know anything.

"I'm just saying it can be pretty scary," Mom said.

"Yeah," I agreed. And for once, I wasn't lying.

"Well, don't let me keep you. If you need any help, let me know."

I pushed past her into my room and shut the door.

I immediately texted Becky.

Max: Sorry I couldn't make it 2day.
Becky: That's cool. Ur friend explained.
Max: Yeah. Cool.
Becky: U know, u don't have 2 b shy.
Max: Just afraid u
    won't like me.
Becky: Why? Do u
    have two heads?
Max: Ha. Just 1.
Becky: Whenever u r
    ready, I'd like 2
    c it.
Max: OK. Soon.
Becky: Don't wait
    2 long. I can't
    b friends with
    somebody who
    doesn't want 2 b round me. L8R Gator.

I looked up from the phone. I thought, What am I going to do now?

My own phone buzzed. It was Karl, sending me a photo of his disguise for Safety Patrol training tomorrow.

Karl's weird. But it's a genius kind of weird.

# CHAPTER 27

Again, it was a great plan. It was an amazing plan. It was an awesome plan. No. It was an AWESOMAZING plan.

I was going to give Becky what she wanted. After school, she was going to finally meet Max. Sort of.

First I had to smooth things over with Molly and Karl. When I got to school, I found them sitting together next to Molly's locker. They didn't look happy.

"This is all your fault." Molly glared.

"What did I do now?" I asked.

"We never found out what scares Roy."

"What happened?" I said.

"We didn't get a picture of the right page," said Karl.

"Remember?" said Molly. "Karl got tangled. *Because you were late.* It took so long to untangle him his phone went dead. *Because you were late.* Mr. Dupree came in before Karl could use your phone. *Because you were late. Because you were too busy with your girlfriend. Because you don't think about anybody but* YOURSELF!"

That's not true. I think about lots of other people. Take Max for example. Sure, he's not real—but when I'm thinking about him, I'm not thinking about me.

"We did get a clue, though," said Karl as he showed me a picture of a page from Roy's file on his phone.

"The tree house!" I said. "Whatever he's afraid of losing, it's in there. We'll check it out together."

"No," growled Molly. "You're not checking out any-thing. Not after yesterday. *We* voted. It's two to one. We're going this afternoon. Karl and me. Alone!"

"Fine!" I said as I fake-stomped away, secretly

thankful I wasn't going. Because *nothing* was going to get in the way of my meeting with Becky.

# CHAPTER 28

After school, while Molly and Karl were checking out Roy's tree house, I followed Becky home.

I did an excellent job avoiding detection.

At least by Becky.

A few blocks from school, she turned and walked the path toward a two-story house. She walked up to the porch and rang the bell. Which was weird. Why would she ring the bell of her own house?

After the door opened and someone let her inside, I slipped behind a fence and started to change.

Just as I finished my transformation into Max, I heard a door slam. I peeked around the fence and saw Becky standing in the backyard. It was now or never. I made my move.

Becky stared at me. "Max?" She said *Max* like it was some sort of alien sand-hopper she just stepped on.

"You were right!" I said. "We can't be friends if we never meet. So, I came to your house."

Becky gasped. It wasn't a scared gasp. It was more like an *Are you kidding me?* gasp. Like the gasp your mom makes when she catches you roasting marshmallows over the gas stove.

Very quietly, Becky said, "This isn't my house."

"Then whose house is it?"

"Becky, is that you?" said a way too familiar Mutant Troll voice from inside the house.

"Ah . . . yeah," squeaked Becky.

"Roy's house!" I whisper-shouted. "This can't be Roy's house. Where's the . . . "

My heart sank to my socks. I stared at Becky. "Then what are YOU doing here?"

"I tutor Roy."

Of course she tutors Roy. She *would* tutor Roy. She's that kind of person—the kind of person that tutors Mutant Troll Bullies.

Becky stared at my alphabet block elevator shoes. "What are you wear—"

"I'm coming out! I've got lemonade!" Roy yelled.

"You've got to hide!" whispered Becky. "Roy *really* doesn't like other people coming to his house. Go. Hide. Now!"

"Hide? Where?" I said.

But Becky took off. I quickly looked around, but there was really only one place to hide.

I stumbled as fast as I could toward the tree house. Somehow I got to the ladder without doing a face-plant. I started to climb.

Just as I got to the top, I felt someone grab my arm and pull me through the door.

It was Molly. Karl lay spread-eagle next to her hugging the tree house floor.

I TOLD YOU I WAS AFRAID OF HEIGHTS.

Molly wasn't happy to see me. "What are

you doing?" she asked. "What is that? An eye patch?"

"Did you poke your eye out running with scissors?" asked Karl, still clutching the floor.

"What? No."

"Oh," said Karl disappointedly. "You shouldn't pretend to have a poked-out eye. It's kind of mean to kids with real poked-out eyes."

"It's a disguise!" I whisper-yelled.

"Disguised as what?" asked Molly.

"It doesn't matter. Just be quiet so Roy doesn't hear us."

Molly continued, "Wait. The only reason you'd come to Roy's house in disguise is to . . ."

"Scare him with your fake poked-out eye!" said Karl.

"It's. Not. A. Fake—"

"To see Becky!" said Molly. "But you're not here as you. So who are you here as?"

"I'm Max! I'm Max! Okay? Now please, shut up!"

"Whoa! You're Max?"

"Who's Max?" asked Karl.

Molly pointed to me. "The kid Roy said he was going to feed to the Cat Dumpster!"

Karl slowly shook his head. "They'll lick your face right off. Their tongues are like little pink sandblasters."

Molly continued, "And Max is the kid who's been text-torturing Roy with his grandmother's phone."

Karl's eyes popped again. "Whoa. You're a fake poked-out-eye double secret agent!"

"Quiet!" I whispered as I looked around for a way out. All I could see was one door and one window. And on the floor next to Molly . . .

"That's that pig from that little kid show," I said. "Is that—?"

STUFFED PIG

"Oinkdexter," said Molly. "And yes, he's Roy's super secret thing from Dr. Daniels's file. If you hadn't shown up, we'd be out of here with him by now."

Before I could figure out what was so special about a stupid stuffed pig, Becky yelled from outside, "Roy, let's just do your homework down here! Not in the TREE HOUSE!"

It was too late. We could hear Roy starting to climb the ladder.

I pointed to the window. "That way! Now!"

Molly and I rushed to the window. But Karl didn't budge.

I turned to Molly. "We've got to go!"

She shook her head. "We're not leaving Karl behind."

We could hear Roy outside. He was almost at the door.

Suddenly Molly yelled at Karl, "By your head! SPIDER!"

"Ahhh!" Karl screamed as he jumped up.

I looked at Molly. "Impressive," I said.

Molly grinned. "How do you think I got Karl up here in the first place?"

Karl rushed toward us and almost threw himself out the window. He'd just made it outside when Molly cried, "The pig!" I quickly reached back in to grab it.

"Hey!" yelled Roy. "What are you . . . ?" Roy stared at Oinkdexter in my hand. "Nooooo!" he screamed.

Roy lunged for me, then fell. He tried to get up, but Becky was holding his leg. "Roy, no! Let Max go!"

"Max? You're Max?" growled Roy.

I didn't answer. I was too busy searching for an escape route. But we were stuck out on a tree limb with nowhere to go. It seemed hopeless, until . . .

A branch overhung the deep end of the pool next door. It was only a seven foot drop, but of course Karl started to panic.

Molly calmly looked into Karl's eyes and said, "Just imagine there are more spiders behind than in front of you."

Karl nodded and immediately started scooting out onto the limb with Molly right behind. The branch sagged under their weight.

I was about to follow when I felt a Mutant Troll hand on my shoulder. Becky yelled, "Max, look out!"

I turned around and came face-to-face with Roy. He grabbed Oinkdexter. "That's mine!"

I held tight to the pig as Roy tried to pull both of us through the window.

"Max, just let him have it," pleaded Becky.

"No!" I grunted. I couldn't let go of the only thing standing between me, Roy, and Roy stuffing me somewhere worse than a locker.

But Roy was too strong. Just as I felt myself about to be dragged through the window I gave one last yank and . . .

Roy gasped and loosened his grip. This was my chance. I braced my feet and lunged backward.

I won! I had the pig! I . . .

All three of us surfaced. My alphabet block elevator shoes made it too hard to swim, so I ripped them off. We swam for the edge, climbed out, and took off.

Behind us, we could hear Roy screaming over and over again, "Oinkdexter! Oinkdexter!"

Roy sounded like he was in real pain. He really wanted that pig back. I almost felt sorry for him.

Almost.

## CHAPTER 29

We ran for blocks and blocks, dripping wet, until we couldn't run anymore, and stopped at a park to catch our breath.

The three of us sat in the swings gasping. Finally, I said, "All in all I thought that went pretty well." Becky and Karl didn't seem to agree.

Molly got up, took Oinkdexter from me, and said, "I'm out of here."

"What are we going to do with the pig?" I asked.

"*We're* not going to do anything," said Molly. "Because *we're* not in Safety Patrol anymore. Because there is no more Safety Patrol."

"Wait. What?"

"We voted. It's two to one and it's over."

I looked at Karl and asked, "When did you vote?"

"C'mon! We can figure something out," I

offered. "I like you guys. I like being in Safety Patrol. All I care about—"

Molly screamed, "IS YOURSELF!"

"Molly, please!" I begged.

Molly ignored me. She turned to Karl. "Are you coming?"

As Molly started to stalk off, Karl turned to me and said, "You know, I was in Safety Patrol before Safety Patrol was cool."

"I know, Karl." I nodded.

"It was a lot more fun then," said Karl.

Karl got off the swing and followed Molly out of the park.

I thought, Fine, be that way. I didn't need them. I could have fun on my own. Like with this swing. Swinging is fun. You don't need any stupid friends to swing. You can swing just fine all by yourself.

So I started to swing.

Slowly at first. Then faster. And higher. And higher. Until I let go.

As I hung there in the air, I looked down and waited for the ground to open up so I could fall. And fall. And fall until I could forget I was falling again.

But the ground didn't open up.

I just fell.

And landed.

And got a face full of dirt.

# CHAPTER 30

I was mostly dry by the time I got home. I tried to squeak-squish past Memaw, but she has eyes in the back of her head. And on her arms. And a few on her legs. And a couple of seriously creepy ones on her feet.

I shook my head. "Nothing."

Memaw frowned. "'Nothing' is as useless as lipstick to a chicken."

"I let some friends down," I said.

"Then pick them up."

YOU LOOK LIKE A BATMAN VILLAIN.

"It's not that easy."

"Are they husky?"

I smiled. "One of them is."

She nodded. "You can't pick your friends up until you pick yourself up."

I shook my head. "I don't understand."

Memaw thought for a second. Then she said, "Let me put it in comic-book terms. You know that one with the spineless kid that fought that gnome that turned everyone to goo?"

"*NanoNerd*, issue fifty three?" I said. "You read *NanoNerd*?"

"You left it in the bathroom," explained Memaw.

"That was a good one," I said. "NanoNerd versus Kew: The Glancing Gnome of Zrew."

NERDOPOLIS
#53 DEC

NANONERD

To
Thine
Own
Self
Be
Goo

Memaw smiled. "A glance from Kew turns nerds to goo."

"Wow." Memaw grinned. "When you tell it, it almost makes sense."

I continued, "In the end, there was only one way for NanoNerd to defeat Kew."

"Yup, the ricochet," said Memaw. "When you hurt your friends you're not going to like what you see when you look in the mirror. You can either stop looking in the mirror and hate yourself forever or . . ."

"Or what?"

Memaw smiled. "Just noodle on it. It'll come to you." Then she leaned over and hugged me.

I noodled on it all evening. I thought pretty much everything could be explained with comic books. But I guess not.

I finally gave up. I was on my way to brush my teeth when Mom stopped me in the hall.

I thought she was going to do her Mom-fu thing and ninja my problem, but instead she said, "I want you to really brush this time. Use the mirror. Make sure you get all the way in the back."

So I did. I brushed the tops and the bottoms. I brushed in front and all the way in the back. I brushed so far back that I bumped that flappy thing that hangs down in the back of your throat.

I gagged. Hard. And coughed. And coughed. And coughed some more.

Mom was at the bathroom door in an instant, saying, "Are you all right?"

"I'm fine. It's okay.

Mom relaxed. She said, "Did you get all the way in the back?"

I nodded.

Mom smiled. "Good boy," she said, then hugged my neck, said, "I love you," and left.

Suddenly I got this weird feeling. Like when somebody says something nice to you, but you know you don't deserve it.

That's when I looked in the mirror, and I knew why I didn't deserve it.

Finally, I understood what Memaw was trying to say. That wasn't me looking back in the mirror. That was Gnick: a Nick/Gnome mutant that lies and lets his friends down. And until I made things right and told the truth, I wouldn't be able to look in the mirror ever again. Without, you know, exploding into goo.

Or something.

I knew what I had to do now. I waited until Memaw fell asleep, then I snatched her phone, and unblocked Roy's number to text him one last time:

Max: Meet me tomorrow at the soccer field at 4.

Finally, I went to bed. But I just lay there. I couldn't sleep. Something was bugging me. Something really, really, super important.

oO HOW COULD KEW AVOID ALL REFLECTIVE SURFACES?

It's not plausible. Water? Metal? Windows? Does everyone live in a bottomless pit on Zrew?

I decided if I survived the next day I was going to send an e-mail to Nerdopolis Comics and demand an answer.

*If* I survived.

# CHAPTER 31

The next morning, I slept in. It was a teacher prep day, so there wasn't any school, just the science fair in the evening.

When I got downstairs, Mom and Memaw had already left. I started to fix some breakfast, when I heard a phone vibrating.

It was Memaw's phone. I picked it up. There was a whole thread of texts from Roy:

Roy: I'll b @ soccer field. U are so dead.
Max: I wouldn't miss it for the world. I'm taking
      you DOWN! Right after my hair appointment.
Roy: ????

I forgot to reblock Memaw's phone last night. Memaw was going to know everything. Which meant that even if I somehow survived Roy,

Becky, Molly, and Karl, there was no way I'd survive Memaw.

$\mathcal{I}$ got to school about an hour before the science fair. I figured that way nobody would be around yet to see me get my spleen ripped out.

I figured wrong.

"'Double, double toil and trouble. Fire burn, and cauldron bubble,'" said Mr. Dupree from behind me.

I turned around and said, "Do *you* even know what the stuff you say means?"

He nodded. "It means I think you, Molly, and Karl are up to something."

Maybe he *is* Emily.

"I know you're anxious to start Safety Patrol. But you're not ready yet. You just need to be patient."

No, he's *not* Emily.

"Speaking of patience, did I ever tell you about the time I was down in Antarctica, training penguins to ski jump for the Olympics?"

No. He's 100 percent not Emily. He's just seriously weird.

"Did you know there's no Olympic participation restriction based on species?"

"Another lie that tells the truth?" I said as I turned back to the field.

"Have you figured that one out yet?" asked Mr. Dupree.

I didn't get a chance to answer because just then I spotted a new hairdo parting the gathering below.

I got to the field, pushed through the crowd, and popped out just in time to hear Memaw say, "I'm looking for a very rude Roy person who's been text-threatening me."

Roy was confused. "Wait. *You're* the one who's been threatening me?"

"Threatening *you*? You're the one who wants to rip out my spleen!" said Memaw.

Roy shook his head. "You *can't* be Max."

I jumped between Memaw and Roy. "No! Stop! I'm Max!"

"You?" said Roy.

"You?" whispered Memaw.

"You!" shouted Becky.

Karl turned to the crowd and pointed to me. "Him."

Memaw grabbed me. "You're the Max that's been bullying this boy?"

I nodded.

Memaw's whole body sagged. Like when all the air leaks out of one of those balloons you see at car dealers.

A girl yelled, "What's going on here?"
Everyone turned to watch the Peer Mediation
Club emerge from the crowd.

I looked at Roy. Roy looked at me. We might
be mortal enemies, but there was one thing we
could agree on: there was no universe, alternate
or otherwise, where we would take our war to
the Peer Mediation Club.

But before we could tell the bossy girls to take
a hike, dozens of cell phones started buzzing at
once.

Everyone checked their phones.

"It says, 'Look up!'" yelled Karl.

And everybody did. Even Roy.

That's when one of Roy's three brain cells decided to randomly click on and he stopped looking up and started looking around.

While everyone was still staring at the sky, Roy grabbed me with one hand and Karl's rolling suitcase backpack with the other. Before I even realized what was happening, Roy had pulled me to the edge of the crowd and started dumping Karl's stuff out of the backpack.

He dumped and dumped and dumped and dumped.

Then he stuffed me in the backpack along with one of Karl's seven tuna pouches and took off.

AND THAT ONE LOOKS LIKE A HAMSTER.

I figured Roy must really like tuna
I figured wrong.

# CHAPTER 33

We bounced along for what seemed like forever, then suddenly stopped. Roy opened the backpack and I quickly figured out the tuna wasn't for him.

It was the Cat Dumpster! Roy was going to smear me with tuna and feed me to the cats!

Seriously, I'd rather have my spleen ripped out.

"Get out!" ordered Roy.

I struggled to stand, then immediately fell over.

I pointed to my legs. "Log legs."

Roy moved toward me. I raised my hands and ducked.

Roy reached past me and grabbed the tuna pouch. "It was you in the tree house in that stupid disguise."

I nodded.

"Where's Oinkdexter?"

"I don't have him."

Roy started to rip open the tuna pouch. "If you don't tell me where he is, you're going in the Dumpster with this on your head."

"I really don't have him. Molly does. And I don't know where!"

I looked up. The Dumpster was now buried in an army of cats, every one of them staring right at me.

I turned back to Roy. "Please. I really don't know! If I did know, I would tell you. I would!"

Roy ripped open the tuna pouch.

"NO!" I screamed.

Roy grabbed me as hundreds of cats licked their lips in anticipation. Then just as Roy raised the tuna pouch over my head . . .

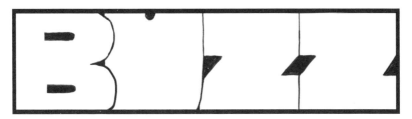

It was Roy's phone. He looked at the screen and gasped. He dropped the phone, fell back against the Dumpster, and slid slowly to the ground. The cats instantly attacked the open tuna pouch still clutched in his hand.

I picked up the phone. It was a text to Roy, from Molly.

Molly: You stop bullying us or the pig gets it!

There was a picture attached.

It was Karl's science fair project, "Will It Twist?" He and Molly were threatening to tear Oinkdexter apart.

I didn't get it. "It's just a stupid stuffed pig," I said. "Why do you . . ."

I looked up from the phone. Roy was still buried in cats fighting over the tuna. He didn't flinch. He just stared into space. And looked . . . wounded.

The Bully in him was gone.

In his place . . .

. . . was a bully I recognized.

# CHAPTER 34

*Y*ou really think you can get Oinkdexter back?" Roy asked. We were standing in the first floor boys' restroom looking up at the access panel to the school's ductwork.

I nodded. "No sweat," I said.

Actually, I had no idea how much sweat it would be. Probably a lot of sweat. Probably more sweat than I could sweat. But I had to help him. I couldn't leave him with those Dumpster cats. Those things can lick the shine off the sun.

"You're sure they won't give Oinkdexter back if I just agree to their terms?" asked Roy.

"I'm sure. If they give him up, what's to stop you from just going back to being a bully?" I explained as I removed the access panel.

"Why are you helping me?" asked Roy.

"So I can look in the mirror."

"What?"

"Forget it. What about you? What's so special about this pig?"

"Oinkdexter smells like my mom."

"Is your mom not around?"

Roy shook his head no.

I didn't know what to say about that, so I didn't say anything for a few seconds. Then I took out my phone and said, "Step one: Beg for help from someone who hates me."

Becky hung up on me. I texted her:

Nick: IT'S NOT ABOUT ME! IT'S ABOUT ROY! I need ur help to get his pig back! Pleez call back!

My phone rang a few seconds later.

"This is all your fault!" Becky shouted.

"Yeah, but we still need your help," I pleaded.

199

"Why are you helping Roy?"

"He asked me to."

"He asked you for help after everything you've done to him? And after everything he's done to you, you said yes?"

"I guess it makes us even," I said.

There was a long pause, and then: "What do I need to do?"

I let out a breath I didn't know I was holding in. Becky didn't completely hate me. Just mostly.

"We've got a half hour," I said. "When I text you, I need you to clear everyone out of the science fair in the cafetorium."

"How am I supposed to do that?"

"I haven't figured that out yet."

"You've really thought this through."

"C'mon, just trust me. Please?"

There was another pause, then she finally said, "Fine."

I hung up and turned to Roy. "Becky's in."

Roy said, "So, we're going to crawl to the ceiling of the cafetorium, somehow clear the science fair, drop down, and grab Oinkdexter."

"See, no sweat."

I immediately started to sweat.

# CHAPTER 35

**R**oy poked his head into the duct and asked, "Are there bugs in here?"

"No. I don't know. Maybe. You're not scared, are you?"

Roy and I entered the duct and started crawling, using my phone as a flashlight.

We passed Dr. Daniels's office and the main office. Everything was going perfectly until . .

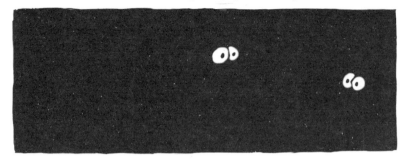

. . . my phone went dead. We couldn't see a thing.

I thought, Don't panic. We still have Roy's phone.

From behind, I could see a dim light come on. Roy said, "Um . . . my battery's almost dead too."

"We'll be fine. Just turn it off. It's just a left, then a right, then a left again. Just follow me."

I crawled forward, feeling my way. After a few feet, I could see light up ahead and hear voices below. We were over the cafetorium. It was just a few more feet to the first vent

"We're here. You okay, Roy?" I asked.

There was no answer.

"Roy?"

I looked back. Roy wasn't there.

"ROY!" I yelled.

"What?" said Roy behind me.

I turned and Roy was suddenly in front of me, on the other side of the vent.

"I never turned my phone back on!" I said. "You must have seen some light from . . ."

"Emily," said Roy.

"Not you too," I said. "You know she's not real!"

"No, she's real. She's real like Oinkdexter is real."

"Oinkdexter is a stuffed pig."

"Oinkdexter helps me deal with stuff I don't understand, just like Emily helps kids deal with stuff they don't understand. If it works, it's real. And it works."

I looked at Roy for a few seconds. Then I said, "You've had a lot of therapy, haven't you, Roy?"

"You have no idea."

Roy turned on his phone. "Ten minutes till the deadline. Have you figured out how you'r going to clear the room?"

"I'm working on it," I said as I peered through the grate at the science fair below. Kids, parents, and teachers were everywhere. There were dozens of exhibits. It was packed. I couldn't see how we were going get everyone out. I was just about to give up when I looked

directly below us and saw the answer staring straight up at me.

I quickly texted Becky.

### RELEASE THE PYTHON!

I hit send. Nothing happened. I stared at the phone, "No bars! We don't have any bars!"

I waved the phone around. It was no use. We had no signal.

Roy took a deep breath. "I'll just agree to the demands," he said. "Thanks for trying."

"They're never going to give you the pig! It's their guarantee you'll keep your promise. There's got to be some other way."

I looked down. Oinkdexter was directly under a vent farther up the duct. If I only had some string or some— I instantly saw what I was looking for.

"Wire!" I said.

Several wires lined the duct. I pulled on one. It wouldn't give.

Roy said, "I'll do it."

He yanked in both directions. The wire came loose. I quickly coiled it up and made a noose with one end.

Roy looked at me. "Five more minutes, and I'm making the deal."

We quickly crawled to the vent overlooking Oinkdexter. I lowered the wire.

Roy grabbed my shoulder. "Please be careful."

I nodded. "I will," I said.

I looked back down. I slipped the noose around Oinkdexter's arm and tightened it. I looked back up at Roy. "Got him."

That's when I felt a yank.

Roy yelled, "She's got Oinkdexter!"

I turned and looked back down and saw Molly tugging on the wire and Becky staring up at us.

Before I could say anything, someone screamed:

A sudden tidal wave of kids and parents fled the python booth for the exits.

I turned to Roy. "Becky must have gotten the message! But how?"

When I turned back, Molly and Becky were gone, overrun by the fleeing crowd.

Roy pointed and yelled, "There! Above the crowd! Oinkdexter!"

We watched helplessly as Oinkdexter disappeared into the stampeding mob.

I looked at Roy. He looked scared. He looked more scared of losing Oinkdexter than I'd ever been scared of him.

# CHAPTER 36

*O*nce the cafetorium cleared, we searched everywhere for the pig. I finally spotted him next to the broken mouse cage. But someone else spotted him too.

"There he is!" Molly and I shouted at the exact same time.

I looked around for Molly and found her and Becky under a table. They were inching toward Oinkdexter. We had to hurry.

But before I could get Roy to lower me down, he pointed below us and screamed, "SNAKE!"

The sight of Willy sliding toward Oinkdexter froze Molly and Becky. I knew pythons were dangerous to mice, not humans, but still, he was a BIG snake. I would have been scared too, if it wasn't for what Roy said next.

"Oinkdexter is all I have left of my mom."

"She's gone?"

"Two years ago."

Suddenly it all made sense. I said, "And he still smells like her."

Roy nodded.

I turned and stuck my legs through the grate. "Lower me down."

Roy grabbed my wrists and lowered me.

I was still too high above the floor. "Just drop me!" I yelled. But Roy wasn't listening. He suddenly let go of one of my wrists, pointed to Oinkdexter and yelled:

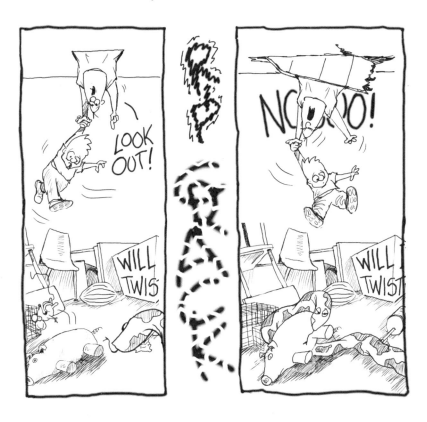

We fell about a foot and stopped. I looked up. The duct had fallen through the ceiling. Roy was stuck in the grate, upside down, holding my arm with a death grip.

Roy yelled, "It's got him!"

I yelled, "Drop me—" but my voice was cut off by a deafening crack as the ceiling gave way and the duct split open.

We were okay. Roy's fall was broken by a watermelon from the "Will It Twist?" exhibit. And my fall was broken by Roy.

We quickly wiped off the watermelon guts, stood up, and came face to face with . . . Karl?

Roy reached for Oinkdexter.

Molly grabbed the pig from Karl. "Not so fast!" she said.

"I promise to stop messing with you guys," said Roy. "Just give me Oinkdexter."

"No way," said Molly. "The pig is our only guarantee you'll keep your promise."

I looked at Roy. "I told you they wouldn't give it up. Let me take care of this."

I walked Molly, Karl, and Becky a few feet away so we could talk alone. I explained how Oinkdexter had a very special smell.

Afterward, we all turned and looked at Roy. He looked smaller for some reason. Almost harmless. Almost.

Molly walked over to Roy and started to hand him the pig, then pulled it back. She said, "No more tying my shoes together or hanging up Karl by his underwear."

"Promise," said Roy.

"And no more stuffing me in my locker," I added.

"What about before gym?" asked Roy.

I had to think about that. "Okay," I said. "But only before gym. And no more shoving me in! I can stuff myself in a locker."

Roy said, "Deal."

Molly, Karl, and I said, "Deal."

Molly handed
Oinkdexter to Roy. Molly,
Becky, and I witnessed the
reunion between boy and
pig. It was awkward to
watch.

"Where's Karl?" asked
Becky.

We turned around and
found him in a power hug with
Willy.

Roy and I quickly uncoiled
Willy and returned him to his
cage.

As we walked back to the
others I asked Roy, "You never
see your mom?"

Roy stopped, smiled, and raised Oinkdexter in
the air.

I SEE HER EVERY DAY!

And that's when I finally understood. Roy didn't see his mother. Mr. Dupree wasn't crazy after all. A lie can tell the truth.

"Ah, guys?" said Karl. "Hey, guys."

Roy and I looked over to see pretty much the entire school staring at us. Standing in front were Dr. Daniels and Mr. Dupree. I couldn't be sure, but I swear Mr. Dupree winked at me.

We all looked at each other. Then we looked back at the crowd and did what all sane kids do when nothing good will come from anything we say.

# CHAPTER 37

Our shrugs cost us all three weeks' detention. Roy and I got weekly bossy-girl Peer Mediation and daily one-on-ones with Dr. Daniels.

Except for the bossy girls, it's not so bad. Those girls really get on Roy's and my nerves. But we can handle it.

The more time I spend with Roy, the more I realize he's not such a bad guy. I'm not saying we're BFFs or anything. I mean, we both have reputations to maintain. He has to occasionally let me stuff myself in my locker. And I have to occasionally call him a tot-brained snot-squid.

Sometimes in detention if none of his snot-squid pals are around, we can talk about stuff. And one thing we talk about a lot is Emily.

A couple of days after the cafetorium thing, as Roy was gently encouraging me into my locker, I showed him texts I got from Becky:

Becky: U did the right thing.
Nick: I wouldn't have been able 2 if you hadn't
     released the python.
Becky: I didn't release the python.
Nick: Who did?
Becky: Emily?

Roy nodded. "Emily's got skills."

"Yeah," I said. "I mean, I get what you said in the ductwork, but that still doesn't make her real."

"Then who released Willy?"

I shrugged. "I checked with Molly. She didn't do it. Karl said he would never take credit for something Emily did. He said it would be rude."

"You're running out of suspects," said Roy.

"That only leaves Mr. Dupree. I thought it was him all along. And then I didn't. And then I thought it HAD to be him, until I made a list of all the Emily stuff that's happened."

EMILY MYSTERIES

AROO! AROO! AROO!

1.) WHO SHOUTED "BRING THE CRAZY"?

2.) WHO TURNED OUT THE LIGHTS IN THE BASEMENT?

3.) WHO TURNED ON THE SPRINKLERS?

4.) WHO SENT THE MASS "LOOK UP" TEXT?

5.) WHO SHINED THE LIGHT THAT LED ROY TO THE RIGHT VENT?

6.) WHO RELEASED THE PYTHON?

"I realized if it were him, he'd be arrested for child endangerment. Mr. Dupree may be crazy, but he's not that crazy."

"You realize that means it couldn't be a teacher or another staff person for the same reason. Dude, Emily's real," said Roy.

"She's a myth," I said as I crawled into my locker. "She's just a story kids make up to explain stuff they can't explain themselves."

"Works for me," Roy said as he shut the locker door. "Later, dude."

Alone, in the dark of my locker, I ran through the Emily suspects again. If it couldn't be an adult, that only leaves a kid who'd have to be supersmart, have the run of the school, and be practically invisible.

That would be a superkid.

# ACKNOWLEDGMENTS

Writing *Geek Guardians: Recess Revolution* has been a pleasure. A pleasure made especially pleasant by the help and support of several key people.

I am deeply indebted to my agent, Dan Lazar. He truly is the hardest-working man in show business. I have never had anyone work as hard on my behalf as Dan has. He is a rock star (without the attitude OR the too tight pants).

This book would be a shell of its present self without the heroic efforts of my fast-talking editor, Lisa Yoskowitz. She has the spooky knack of knowing where I want to go before I want to go there. I am eternally grateful for her patience, intelligence, and making me look like a way better writer than I am. Oh . . . and I'm also grateful for her laugh—always at just the right time.

A big thank-you to Marci Senders for the terrific job she did designing the cover, as well as for her patience with lost files, wrong-resolution art, and my inability to render a brave yet mischievous expression.

A thank-you to everyone at Disney • Hyperion who helped make this book come to life and somehow miraculously get into readers' hands. I think magic elves were involved. I'm not sure.

Thank you to friends Halley, Thomas, Sarah, Jeff, Cyndy, Bozena, Tutta, Kara, Dan, Bill, Ces, Sue, Roy and Neva. It takes a village to make an idiot. Or something.

I'd like to thank my family as well. My daughters, Sarah and Emily, both read early drafts and didn't once throw up or laugh in my face. They each, however, did make constructive comments using the words "lame," "gross," and just occasionally "awesome." My wife, Kim, a veteran at dealing with my insecurities and neuroses, specializes in the loving fake laugh. I know it's fake. She knows it's fake. It doesn't matter. It's a laugh. And she knows that sometimes it's exactly what I need. And she's right. She's always right.

Finally, I want to thank my mom. She read every draft. She followed every twist and turn on the path to publication. She listened and encouraged and cheered. I'm so thankful that I was able to share this journey with her. And even though she's my mom and she's supposed to love everything I do, I'm pretty sure she really, really likes this book. But not as much as her San Francisco Giants.

Let's not get crazy here.

# MICHAEL FRY

spent middle school as a geeky, nerdy Chess Club member who played the French horn—and survived (mostly intact).

His school days behind him, Mike is the co-creator and writer of several comic strips, including *Over the Hedge*, which is featured in newspapers nationwide and was adapted into the hit animated movie of the same name. In addition to working as a cartoonist, Mike is the co-founder of RingTales, a company that animates print comics for all digital media, and is an active blogger, tweeter, and public speaker, as well as the proud father of two adult daughters.

Originally from Minneapolis, Mike currently lives with his wife in Austin, Texas, where he is hard at work on the next *Geek Guardians* adventure.